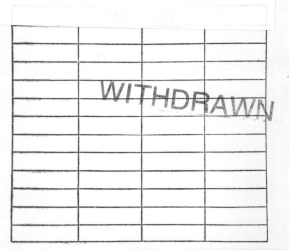

A TIME
FOR
HANGING

A TIME
FOR
HANGING

BILL CRIDER

Thorndike Press • Thorndike, Maine

Library of Congress Cataloging in Publication Data:

Crider, Bill, 1941-
  A time for hanging / Bill Crider. -- Large print ed.
    p. cm.
  ISBN 1-56054-002-8 (alk. paper : lg. print)
  1. Large type books. I. Title.
[PS3553.R497T5   1989b]   90-34619
813'.54--dc20   CIP

Thorndike Press Large Print edition published in 1990 by arrangement with M. Evans & Company, Inc.

Cover design by James B. Murray.

The tree indicum is a trademark of Thorndike Press.

This book is printed on acid-free, high opacity paper.

For Harry Whittington
A Writer's Writer

Chapter One

Paco Morales had seen the woman before, had seen her often, really, at least for the past month or so, despite the fact that his mother would always send him out of the shack when the woman was there.

"Paco," his mother would say, "go and draw up a bucket of water and give it to the mule."

Paco would dutifully go outside and lower the wooden bucket into the old well, the pulley creaking as the rope slid through it. When the bucket hit bottom with a splash, he always waited a long time for it to fill, longer than really necessary. Then he pulled it slowly back up, reached across the rim of the well, and pulled the bucket to him, hardly ever spilling a drop. Then he poured that water into another bucket and took that one to the mule.

The mule hardly ever wanted to drink. The woman never came except late in the evenings, and by then most of the heat of the day was gone. Paco's bare feet could still feel it in the hard-packed dirt, but the night air was cool and there was nearly always a slight breeze.

Still, it was Paco's job to make the mule drink, or to wait until it did. By the time he got back to the house the woman was always gone. Paco's mother never said what it was that the woman had wanted, and Paco never asked. There were some things his mother never discussed, and her visitors were one of those things.

They often gave her money, which Paco knew was important to the family, especially so since his father had been killed by a gringo in a card game. The gringo had accused Paco's father of cheating, though Paco knew that his father would never have done such a thing.

It didn't matter what Paco thought, however. Everyone else was quite ready to believe that the gringo was telling the truth and that Paco's father had died the way a cheater should — shot through the heart with a .44-caliber slug.

Paco had tried to be a man for his mother and sisters since that time. He was, after all, fifteen years old now and could do as much work as any man. His shoulders were wide, and they strained at the seams of his father's old shirts. The frayed legs of the stained and faded Levi's stopped far above his ankles, and his hands were broad and strong.

His mother had not let him go out into the

world, though. He had been forced to stay around the little farm, plowing with the mule, doing the planting, fetching the water. They had a cow, too, and some chickens, so with what they could grow and take in from the visitors they managed to get by.

This was one visitor that would not be coming again, Paco thought as he gazed down at her. He hardly recognized her now.

Her dress was ripped and torn, and it bunched about her waist. Her legs were twisted back under her, and her head was lying at a very strange angle. There was blood on her face.

In the moonlight, her legs were pale and white, and Paco suddenly wished that he had taken some other way home that evening. Fear stabbed at him, churning his stomach, yet he could not tear himself away from the sight.

He had gone to town for a little salt and a bit of sugar from Tomkins' Store, but he had long since forgotten that he held the twists of paper in his hand.

He had never seen a dead woman before, not like this.

He had been late because he had stopped to talk to Juanito García for a few minutes, and dusk had crept up on them unnoticed. So he had taken a shortcut home, off the main road and over a little-used trail through a thick grove of trees.

He could no longer even remember what he and Juanito García had said to one another.

All he could think of was the dead woman.

She had been beautiful when she visited his mother, or so she had seemed to Paco, her red hair shining in the lamplight of the shack.

It was not shining now.

Go home, Paco thought. *I must go home.*

But he couldn't move. His feet seemed rooted to the ground as he stood in the grove of trees, looking at the body lying in front of him.

He might not have seen her if it hadn't been for the noise. She wasn't exactly right on the trail, but off a little way, hidden in the brush.

Paco had heard something as he walked along, something like the cry a small animal might make if it was trapped or afraid. He liked animals, and he thought he might help it if he could. There was nothing to be afraid of this close to town, nothing more than a squirrel, he thought. Perhaps a deer.

The sound came from somewhere down the trail, and when he got to the spot he thought was about right, he began looking for the source of the noise, peering through the gloom of tangled branches and thick leaves.

He wasn't thinking about how late it was,

or that his mother would be worried about him. He was thinking about some poor animal in distress.

He caught sight of the woman's dress, and he realized that it was not an animal that he had heard. There was no animal of that color in all the country. He made his way to the bundle of color that had caught his attention and found the woman.

He didn't even know her name, he realized. His mother never mentioned the names of her visitors.

He wondered who he should tell.

Then he wondered if the killer was still around. He looked over his shoulder so quickly that his neck popped, but there was no one there. Whoever had killed the woman was long gone.

Another thought came to him, the most frightening thought of all. What if they thought he killed her?

They would, of course.

"They" were the ones who had stood by when his father was murdered and said nothing. Nothing good, that is.

They said things like, "That'll teach the greaser to cheat a white man at cards."

Or, "How many men you killed, Hank?" — Hank being the offended gambler's name — "not countin' Meskins, o'course."

Or, "Hell, Hank, you had to kill him. He was cheatin'. Hell, yes. That's just what comes of lettin' a Meskin play cards with white men. We shoulda known better."

They were the same ones who, if they got the chance, would say that Paco had killed the woman.

Well, he wasn't going to give them the chance. He was going to get out of there. Right now. He willed his feet to move, and this time they obeyed him.

He turned back to the trail, and now the noises of the evening that were normally so unthreatening became magnified and frightening to him.

From far off in the grove there came the cry of an owl, and that call was echoed by the voice of some other night bird that Paco could not identify.

Or perhaps it was not a bird.

Something scurried through the brush at his feet, making a sudden rush from one place of concealment to another.

Paco began to run.

The trail, when he came to it, was rough and hard. It had not rained for several weeks, and the ground had been churned by horses' hooves when it was last muddy, making it very uneven. He stumbled along as fast as he could, the hard ground bruising his feet.

He thought he heard something at his back, and he veered off the trail into the trees, panic causing his heart to pump faster. What if there was someone behind him?

He was almost too afraid to look back.

The tree branches lashed at his face, and he put out his hands to keep them away. He had dropped the sugar and salt long ago, but he did not remember doing it.

He was sure there was someone behind him now, and his fear and panic increased. What if they caught him? They would show him no mercy, no more mercy than his father had received.

He conquered his fear momentarily and looked back over his shoulder, a mistake. He should have kept his eyes to the front. He ran headlong into a tree.

For a few seconds he felt nothing; then he felt only the throbbing of his head as pain washed through it like a fast-moving stream.

He could no longer hear the hoofbeats, if he had ever heard them. He could not hear anything.

He fell face forward on the ground.

Chapter Two

The Reverend Wayne Randall wondered where his daughter was. She had been acting strangely lately, going off with no warning and coming back in time for supper. Such behavior was very unlike Elizabeth. She had made it a habit to be around the house to help her mother with the meals, but now her unexplained absences had become more frequent, and she had not responded obediently to his questions, refusing obstinately to answer him when he asked about her whereabouts.

Tonight the table had been set for over an hour, and Randall's wife, Martha, had tried to keep the meal warm.

Finally she had to speak. "I don't believe our daughter's coming home for supper."

Randall was sitting at his place at the head of the table, as was right for the man of the family. His head was bowed over his plate, but he looked up at his wife's words.

He tried to keep the distaste he felt for her

14

out of his voice. "Sharper than the serpent's tooth," he said.

Immediately, his wife teared up. He knew that she hated for him to talk like that about Elizabeth, but he didn't care. He had long since stopped caring one way or the other about what she thought. He knew it wasn't Christian, but he couldn't help himself. He had prayed about it, to no avail.

It was the way she looked. When they had married, she had been slim and fair, hair as red as fire, but something had happened to her, something that he hated but could not prevent.

She had changed.

After the birth of their child, she had become larger and larger, turning to soft fat before his eyes. Her arms were as big around as his own thighs, or so it seemed to him, white and thick as bread dough. He often thought that if he stuck a finger in her, it would leave a dimple.

He never tested the theory, however. He had long since ceased to touch her, and she had long since ceased to care.

She looked at him across the table, her little faded eyes almost blurred in folds of fat, the tears squeezing out of them.

"You don't even care about your daughter," she said. Even her voice irritated him.

It was high and whiny.

"I care," he said, feeling the anger rising in him, the way it always did.

"You've mistreated her, mishandled —"

"That's enough!" Randall roared, standing abruptly, shoving the table away from him, rattling the dishes. He was an imposing man, corpulent, with an impressive hard belly. He was dressed, as usual, in black, except for his white shirt. His tie, which he wore from morning until bedtime, was also black.

"I have done my best for that girl," he said, biting off the words and spacing them for emphasis. "I have always done my best."

He reached for the Bible which sat on the table by his plate. He always had a Bible close at hand.

When he picked it up, he gripped it in his right hand and held it to his breast. "I have raised her by this book, and by God's words. Any mistakes that have been made —"

"No!" Martha said, and she too stood up. She was not tall, no more than five feet and a few inches, which emphasized her bulk. "I won't allow you to say that again."

Randall was dumbfounded. His wife was a woman who knew her place. That was one of her only good qualities. She never contradicted him; she always did his bidding and performed her wifely duties around the house

16

without protest or complaint.

There were no tears in her eyes now. She pressed the advantage of his surprise. "You've been hard with her, too hard. Whatever she is, you made her that way."

"Woman, you forget yourself," he sputtered.

"No," she said. "I'm remembering."

He looked at her blankly.

"I'm remembering how you treat her, always. Not the way you treat me, not that way, but almost as bad."

"I don't know what you mean," Randall said, putting all the self-righteousness he could into his tone as he continued to clutch his Bible to him.

"Of course you know," his wife said. "You've never let her lead a normal life, not the way a girl should."

"I am a man of God," he said, more self-righteous than ever. "A normal life is not for me and mine."

"I don't mean it the way you do," she said. "The kind of life you're talking about, well, I guess I accepted that when I married you. I knew that we'd never have much money, that we'd have to live on what we could take in from the church members, whether it was money or chickens or ear corn. That we'd have to live with cast-off furniture in a house that none of the members would want for themselves but that they think's just fine for their preacher."

She paused for breath, but Randall didn't try to say anything. He couldn't *think* of anything to say, though his face was contorted with the effort.

"It's the other things," Martha went on. "Always making her sit in the front row of the church every Sunday morning, not letting her even move or wiggle so much as a toe without leaning down out of that pulpit and yellin', 'That's the devil in you, Lizzie! Sit still and shame the devil.'"

"The Lord our God demands a reverent heart," Randall said.

"And every time a boy'd come around to play, it was off with Lizzie to her room or to her chores. No time for that, you'd say. Not even when she got older, and the boys'd be around her like bees around a honeycomb. You never gave her a chance to let one of them come calling, not ever. Whenever she'd ask, you'd turn it around, make it sound like whoever it was that wanted to come by, even if it was just for a little talk, was burning with all the lusts of Sodom."

Randall pulled himself straighter, pulled the Bible closer to his breast and held it there like a shield.

"That time you found her sitting under the

sycamore tree on Sunday afternoon with the Collins boy. You pulled her away from there as if he was the imp of Satan himself, pulled her right back of the house and took off your belt and —"

Randall slammed the Bible down on the table. The plates and forks jumped into the air and clattered down.

"Woman!" he yelled. "You've said too much. Wives must be subservient to their husbands —"

"And so I have been, for far too long!" she stormed at him. "Where has it gotten me?" She looked down at herself and the tears spurted from her eyes again. "Look where it's gotten me. Look what you've made me."

"I've made you nothing," he said coldly. "What you are is your own doing."

"No," she said. "But that doesn't matter. It's what you've made of Elizabeth that matters."

"And what might that be?"

"I don't know." With these words, the spirit seemed to go out of her. "I just don't know. But she's secretive now, the girl who used to tell me everything. She sneaks out of the house at all hours —"

"What?"

"Oh, it's been going on for a while. I knew, but I didn't say anything. I didn't want to have you beat her again."

"Spare the rod and spoil the child," Randall said sententiously.

"I'm almost certain you believe that, and that's why I didn't tell you. Then she got bolder, or more desperate, and left even when you knew. But she never said why."

Randall picked up his Bible again and twisted it in his hands. The leather cover creaked. "If it was a man . . ."

"If it was, what will you do? For all you know she's with him now, and she may never come back."

Randall shuddered as if from a sudden chill.

"She'll be back," he said. "You'll see. She'll be back."

But somehow there was no force in his words. Martha could tell that he wasn't sure. For the first time in his life, he wasn't sure that he was right, and he was clearly shaken.

It must be a terrible thing, she thought, for a man who's always known he's right, known it for nearly fifty years, to suddenly think he might be wrong. And if he's thinking back over those years for the first time, really thinking, to realize that he might have been wrong before, and been wrong more than once.

Seeing the stricken look in his eyes, she almost wanted to walk around the table that

separated them and take him in her arms. Almost. But she couldn't bring herself to do it.

They stood there like that, staring at one
another like strangers.

Chapter Three

Fireflies filled the grove, flickering and shimmering in the darkness.

Paco sat up and shook his head, and the fireflies disappeared. He realized that they had never actually been there. They had been nothing more than dazzle left behind by the solid blow on his head he had received from the tree.

The night was quiet now; there was not even the call of the owl to disturb the silence.

Paco got to his feet, putting his hand against the tree trunk to steady himself. His head throbbed painfully, and everything seemed to be whirling around him. He could taste blood in his mouth.

He stood there for a few minutes, trying to remember what had happened. Then it all came back to him in a rush — the dead woman, his sudden panic, his collision with the tree. He had no idea how long he had lain on the ground, or how late it might be, but he knew that he had to get out of there. The blow on his head had done one good thing for him: he was no longer afraid.

The full moon was high in the sky, and quite a bit of its mellow light filtered through the tree branches, shadowing the ground at Paco's feet. He looked around helplessly for the salt and sugar he had been holding at one time, but they were nowhere to be seen.

He felt his fear returning, but he controlled the urge to run. There was no need to hurry. He was alone, except for the woman, and the woman would not be bothering him. He would retrace his steps and try to find the sugar and salt. He must have dropped them in his headlong flight. If he was careful, he would be able to find them. He hoped they had not spilled.

He began walking back the way he had come, looking at the ground as carefully as he could in the dark. He had almost reached the trail when he heard voices.

He stepped back into the trees, pressing himself to the trunk of a large elm. The sharp point of a broken limb poked him through his thin shirt.

At first the voices were just a blur, but then he began to distinguish them. There were obviously a number of men, all of them talking loud.

"Dammit, Harl, watch out where you're

goin'," someone said. "This trail's too narrow for more than one of us."

Harl, Paco thought. That would be Harl Case, the owner of the livery stable, the only man in town by that name. What was he doing there?

"All right, I'm a-movin'," Harl said. "We got to spread out anyway if we're gonna find anybody around here. Myself, I think we're chasin' all over the territory for nothin'. That girl's got clear of this town and her daddy, and I don't blame her."

"Damn right," the first man said. "He's had her on such a tight rein, I expect she's high-tailed it. Wouldn't be surprised to find out there's some young fella missin', too. Hell, if I was young enough, I'd've run with her myself."

"That'd be the day, Jack Simkins," a third voice said. "Even if you was young, you're so ugly a blind mule wouldn't run off with you."

There was the sound of laughter.

"On second thought, maybe I could be wrong about that. A blind mule might be 'xactly the kinda thing that'd catch your eye."

Paco knew Jack Simkins, or knew who he was. He was the sheriff's deputy, a big, lazy man with a glass eye and a scarred face. He

24

was ugly, all right, but everybody liked him. He was easygoing and good-natured, but that didn't matter to Paco right then. He didn't want to be found by anybody, no matter how good-natured. It was easygoing men like Simkins who had stood by when his father was killed and let the gambler go free.

He heard the men crashing through the brush as they continued to call back and forth to one another. He thought that maybe he could make a run for it. They were making so much noise that they weren't likely to hear him.

He didn't know for sure how many of them there were, but he figured that there were about six. Five for sure. He moved stealthily from the shelter of the tree trunk, bending low to the ground and staying in the shadows.

He had not gotten far when he heard someone cry out. "Jesus Christ a'mighty!"

"What is it, Len?" Harl yelled. "What's the matter?"

"I found her, fellas. God a'mighty, I found her! Get over here, quick!"

The sounds of the crashing around increased as the other men ran to where Len Hawkins was. Hawkins was the owner of a hardware store, a rail-thin man with no hair at all on his head. Paco had often wondered just how old Len Hawkins was. His wrinkled bald head made him look ancient, but his eyes were young, and the skin of his face was like that of a young girl.

Paco began moving faster. There was no way, in all their excitement, they could hear him now.

But suddenly everything grew quiet, and Paco had to halt. The men had come to the body, and Paco could hear them cursing under their breath.

Finally Len Hawkins spoke aloud. "I can't believe this, I just can't believe it," he said. "It's Lizzie Randall, sure as hell. Who'd do a thing like this, fellas? Who?"

No one answered him for a while. Paco knew what they were feeling, the same mixture of fear and awe that he himself had felt not so long ago.

It was not so much that the woman was dead. The men could have accepted that, as could Paco. Death was a fact of life that all of them had come to accept early on. Too many babies died, too many men got snake-bit or thrown from bucking horses or shot in saloons for death to be frightening in itself.

It was the way of this death that was shocking.

Women were, for the most part, respected and honored by all the men. Paco knew that there were exceptions, like the women that

26

worked for Mr. Danton in the saloon, but the dead woman was not one of those.

Even those women were treated with a kind of special deference by most men of the town.

So to find a woman like this, dead in the trees, obviously killed by someone strong, probably in a hard struggle, was shocking.

It was even more shocking to the men who gathered round her now than it had been to Paco, for they knew who she was.

"It's the preacher's daughter, all right," Jack Simkins said. "I'd know that red hair of hers anyplace."

"What the hell's she doin' out here, anyways?" Harl Case wondered. "Woman's got no business wanderin' off into a place like this."

"Well, she's been here before," Jack said. "That's why Sheriff Vincent sent us out here in the first place. He said somebody'd seen her walking this trail more'n once."

"What're we gonna do?" Len Hawkins asked. "Who's gonna tell her pa?"

"Seems to me that's the sheriff's job," said a voice Paco did not recognize. "I sure as hell ain't gonna be the one."

"We'll let him decide that," Jack said. "The rest of you men stand guard here. I'll go back to town and let the sheriff know about this."

"You better tell him to get a rope ready,"

27

Harl said. "Whoever done this is gonna swing for it, and that's the truth."

Paco didn't wait for Jack's reply to that. He started making his way through the trees again.

He might have made it to safety if he hadn't hooked his foot in a sharp-thorned vine that grew near a tree. He fell forward, trying to stifle the yell that escaped his lips as the fire raked his shins through the worn Levi's.

"What the hell's that?" Jack Simkins said.

"Somebody's out there!"

"Let's get the son of a bitch!"

There was more crashing and thrashing of tree branches as the men began storming toward the spot where Paco lay.

He tore his way free of the vine and got to his feet. His head was throbbing again; he could feel the blood pounding in it. The fall had not done him any good.

He could hardly move, much less run. He put out his hands and stumbled blindly forward.

Shots rang out and he could hear the bullets clipping the branches nearby.

He stopped in his tracks and turned to face the charging men. "It is only me, Paco Morales," he called out, hoping that he could avert their fury by letting them know that he was harmless.

They did not care who he was. They were horrified by what they had seen, and they were not thinking rationally at all. They wanted to hurt someone, to make someone pay, and Paco was there.

He was going to pay.

They stopped shooting when they saw that he was not going to run, but when they caught up with him they began raining blows on him, smashing his face with their fists, mashing his lips and causing the blood to fly, breaking his teeth, hammering his chest and sides until he fell to the ground, and then kicking him repeatedly after he had fallen.

Fortunately for Paco, he did not know most of what was happening to him. He had screamed at first and tried to defend himself, but after the first few fists had struck his head like blocks of wood, he had lost consciousness.

After a few minutes the men stopped beating him. They were tired and out of breath from the effort, and they looked at one another, their heads hanging, somewhat ashamed of what they had done, but nevertheless sure that they had been right.

"He's the one that done it," Len Hawkins said, panting slightly as he massaged his left hand with his right. He thought he might have broken a knuckle. "You think we killed him?"

"Naw, he's alive," Harl Case said. "He

won't last long, though, when folks find out what he's done."

"We don't know for sure he done anything," Jack Simkins reminded them, a little worried about the beating.

"Now wait a minute," Turley Ross said. His had been the voice Paco had not recognized. He was short and stocky, with broad shoulders and long arms. He had gotten in a number of good licks on Paco, and he knew the boy deserved them. "We know he done it. He killed that girl back there, and no tellin' what else he done to her."

They all thought about that for a minute.

"Well," Simkins said slowly, "he was here, all right. But that don't mean he done anything."

They looked down at the boy who lay at their feet. He was breathing, but that was all they could say for him. One of his arms looked funny, probably broken, and he had been kicked plenty hard. Maybe a few ribs broken, too.

And his face wasn't going to be pretty. Even in the dark, they could see that it looked like a side of raw beef.

"Hell, he done it. Why else would he be here, and then try to sneak off?" Lane Harper asked. Harper was the fifth man in the group, a bartender in Danton's Saloon. He was a big man with a black mustache and thinning black hair that he combed in long strands across his balding skull.

Simkins tried to think, which was not his strong point. But he was the representative of the law here, and he wanted to do things right.

"He could've done it, that's for sure," he finally said.

"Could've, my ass," Harl said. "He's the one done it, and that's that. We practically caught him in the act, and we captured him. Hell, folks are gonna thank us for what we done when we bring him in."

"Paco Morales is who he is," Harper said. "It was his daddy that got shot over that card game a few years back. A cheatin' greaser. Things like that run in the blood. Now his boy's turned killer."

The men remembered the card game. They also remembered that there had been some talk around town that Roberto Morales, Paco's father, had not been cheating at all. In fact, so the talk had gone, it was that tinhorn gambler — Hank something or other — who had done the cheating and Morales had called him on it. But it was Morales who ended up dead, and there wasn't much more said about it, Morales being a Mexican. And the men certainly weren't going to bring up the question of his innocence now. It was best that no one mention it.

Paco stirred.

"He's comin' around," Simkins said. "We got to do something with him."

"We got to take him to the damn jail, is what we'll do," Hawkins said. "Then he'll get a fair trial before we hang him. Least he might get a trial. There'll be some want to hang him sooner."

Simkins still didn't like it. He knew that there was the little matter of proof, of evidence, of which they had none except for Paco's presence there, but the others all seemed convinced that Paco had to be guilty of the girl's death.

If he wasn't guilty, would they have savagely beaten him the way they had done?

Of course not.

They had half killed him, so he must be guilty. That was the only way to justify their actions.

"All right, then," Simkins said. "A couple of you can stay here with him, and the other two can go stand by the body. Turley, you and Harl can do that. I'll go tell the sheriff what's happened and get a wagon so we can take 'em back to town."

"Maybe we oughta just hang him ourselves," Turley said.

"What?" Simkins said. "Hang him?"

"Why the hell not? He done it." Turley was defensive and angry. "God damn Meskin killin' a white woman like that. I say we get a rope and hang him right here on the spot."

"We can't do a thing like that," Simkins said.

"Sure we can," Turley said. "Save the judge some trouble."

"Turley's right," Harl said. "We can do it ourselves. Wouldn't nobody say anything against it. What do you say, Lane?"

Harper, like the others, was thinking about what had happened. They had viciously beaten the boy, who was practically dead already.

What if he got to be all right before the judge got him tried. What if he was able to convince a jury that he didn't have anything to do with the killing? What would that make the men who had beaten him? It could make them not much better than killers themselves, that's what.

On the other hand, if the boy was dead, he wouldn't be able to say anything at all.

"I say we hang him," Harper said.

"I'll go along with that," Hawkins added.

"Well, it ain't gonna be that way," Jack Simkins said. "I ain't much of a lawman, but I'm enough of a one to know better than to stand still for a lynchin', even if it is a Meskin."

He drew his pistol. "So I guess I'm gonna have to be the one to stay here and watch this boy and let one of you go get the sheriff. Turley, that might's well be you. And you others can go and stand down there by the girl. I don't need no help here."

"You don't need to treat us like this, Jack," Lane Harper said. "We didn't mean no harm."

"You meant to hang this boy here."

"It's just that he ought to hang," Harl said. "Look what he done to that girl."

"That's as may be. Right now we ain't entirely sure of that."

"I'm sure," Hawkins said.

"Me, too," Turley said.

"I'd hate to have to shoot you boys over something like this," Jack said. He had kept the barrel of his pistol pointed down. Now he raised it slightly. "Turley, you ride on back to town for the sheriff like I said. Lane, you might's well go with him and bring the doc."

"God damn, Jack —"

"That's enough of that, now. Go on."

For a minute Jack thought they might rush him. They stood there looking at him, breathing hard, their fists opening and closing, but the moment passed. They turned and walked away, leaving him standing there, the boy at his feet.

Jack looked down at the motionless Paco. "I'll say one thing, boy. If you had any shoes on, I'd sure hate to be in 'em right now."

He holstered his pistol and leaned back against a tree to wait for the sheriff.

Chapter Four

Sheriff Ward Vincent had never wanted to be the law in Dry Springs. He had stood for election only because no one else would do it after the last sheriff, old Frank Rawlings, had been killed one night by a liquored-up young gunsharp who'd been hoorawin' the town, shooting out windows and scaring people half to death. The gunman had got clean away, and no one had ever seen him again. Five or six months went by before an election was held, because it took that long to get someone to say he'd run.

That had been seven years ago, and Vincent had been the sheriff ever since, doing the best job he could for fifty dollars a month. He didn't have a family to support, his wife having died of a fever so early in their marriage that they'd never had children, so the money was all right; and to tell the truth, the job wasn't as bad as it might have been. Just the usual drunks, an occasional fight at Danton's Saloon, now and then a little robbery, but nothing to cause a man to lose his sleep.

So it wasn't the job itself that bothered Vincent. Instead, it was the constant thought of what *might* happen that kept him in a sweat. He knew he wasn't a brave man, though after seven years people had started thinking of him that way.

You wear the badge long enough, and people begin to think you've got the guts to back it up. Break up a fight or two, run a couple of rowdies out of town, and people begin to believe you're a handy man with your fists or a gun.

Vincent wasn't any of those things. He was just an ordinary man who had to do his job as best he could. He'd never been tested in a really tough situation. The nearest he ever came was the time Roberto Morales got shot, and the gambler had claimed self-defense. Said Morales was cheating and when the gambler called his hand, Morales came at him with a knife. So the gambler shot him.

A couple of folks backed the gambler up. Lane Harper, for one. Said he'd seen the whole thing, and sure enough, there was a knife lying there by Morales's body, a huge pigsticker that no one in town ever remembered seeing Morales carry.

Nobody could ever remember Morales being anything but honest, either, but the gambler went on his way without much question.

Vincent thought about it every now and then, as he thought about it now, sitting in the little hot-box of a jail, looking up at the round-faced clock on the wall.

Eleven o'clock. Not that late if it was a Saturday night, but nothing ever happened in Dry Springs on a Tuesday, which is what it was now. Vincent was only rarely awake this late during the middle of the week.

He opened the top drawer of the scarred old desk and rummaged around in it for the winding key, found it, and walked over to the clock. He opened the face, inserted the key, and gave it a couple of turns. The spring was already tight, so he put the key back in the desk.

He sat back down and thought about Lizzie Randall.

Her father had been all in a sweat, saying that his daughter had disappeared.

That had been two hours earlier.

"What do you mean, 'disappeared,' Preacher?" Vincent said.

"I mean she's gone," Randall said. "She left the house, and she hasn't come back for supper. My wife . . ." He paused. "My wife's worried sick."

"She ever go off before?"

Randall straightened. He swallowed twice, his prominent Adam's apple bobbing up and down. "Never," he said, his mouth dry as he tried to swallow the lie.

That wasn't what Vincent had heard. As the sheriff, he kept a close eye on the town and knew a lot more about what went on than nearly anyone. He knew more about Lizzie Randall than her parents did, he suspected.

"Well, now," he said, "where do you think she might be gone?"

"I have no idea," Randall said. "I thought that was your job. To find her."

"I'll send some men out to look for her," Vincent said. "I don't reckon she's gone too far."

He already had in mind a couple of places for the men to search. He knew that Lizzie had been in the habit of straying around the town after dark lately. That was no surprise, considering the way Randall kept her hobbled. Vincent suspected that she was meeting a young man. He hated to break up a rendez-vous, but it was late, after all, and time for her to be getting home. She'd probably just lost track of the time.

"You go on home," he told Randall. "I'll take care of things. We'll have her back before you know it."

Randall appeared reluctant to leave.

"Shouldn't I stay here and wait until you find out something?"

"There's no reason for that," Vincent reassured him. "Jack'll be in any minute, and I'll have him round up a few men to look for your daughter. They'll find her. Don't worry about that."

"Well," Randall said hesitantly, "if you say so, I suppose it's all right."

"You can count on it," Vincent said.

"You'll let us know as soon as you find her?"

"That's what I've been tellin' you."

Randall left then, but he was clearly not happy with the situation. It seemed to Vincent almost as if the preacher didn't want to go back home.

He had not been gone long before Jack came in.

"Town's quiet, Sheriff," he said. "Not much stirrin' around tonight." He smiled, which had the effect of making his face a bit less grotesque. He was always glad to report a quiet evening. He didn't like action any better than Vincent did.

"We do have one little problem," Vincent told him. He filled him in on Randall's visit.

"Damn," Jack said. "You know, a few nights back I thought I saw her over to that grove of trees on the west side of town. That was earlier than this, though."

"I remember," Vincent said. "I don't think there's anything to this, but we might as well do it right. Anybody still over at the saloon?"

"A few," Jack said.

"Well, round 'em up and get 'em out lookin'. Send a few over to the springs, and you take the rest over to the woods. If we don't locate her there, we'll try something else. I expect she'll be home before you hardly get to lookin'."

"All right, Sheriff," Jack said. "You want me to bring her in if I find her?"

"That's the idea. I'll give her a little lecture on not worryin' her daddy, and we'll let it go at that."

Chapter Five

Vincent looked at the clock again.

Eleven-fifteen.

He was beginning to wonder why Jack hadn't come back when he heard horses outside. The door banged open and Turley Ross came in.

"Howdy, Sheriff," Ross said.

"Howdy, Turley. You one of the search party?"

"Yeah. We found her."

"Good," Vincent said, getting out of his chair. "Where —"

"We found the son of a bitch that killed her, too," Ross said.

Vincent felt as if someone had hit him in the kidneys with a three-foot club. "Wait a minute, Turley, what're you —"

"It was that Paco Morales," Turley went on. "Meskin kid that lives in a shack out past the edge of town. He's the one done it."

Vincent took a deep breath and tried to steady his nerves. "Lizzie Randall," he said.

"You tellin' me she's dead?"

"Damn right, she's dead. Raped, too, probably, you ask me. It was that Meskin kid, like I said. Lane Harper's gone for the doc."

Vincent sat on the edge of his desk, trying to take it in. He could feel his sweaty shirt sticking to his back. "You're sure she's dead?"

"Hell, you oughta see her. She's dead all right." Ross shook his head. "Damn shame, too, her daddy bein' the preacher and all."

Vincent could hardly believe what he was hearing. Lizzie Randall, dead. And killed by the same boy whose father had been shot in the only other incident that had disturbed Vincent's more or less peaceful career as sheriff of Dry Springs.

"You say you caught him red-handed?"

"Damn right we did. We shoulda strung him up on the spot, you ask me. Throwed a rope over one of them tree limbs out there and hung him like the murderin' bastard he is."

The lawman in Vincent took over. "You can't do things that way, Turley. This is a law-abidin' town. We don't go in for lynchin'."

"Wouldn't be lynchin', exactly. Hell, we caught him in the act."

"How'd he kill her?"

"Don't know that. Guess the doc'll have to tell us."

43

"I thought you caught him in the act."

Turley shook his head and looked stubborn. "We did, kind of. We caught him tryin' to get away, and that's the same thing. There just ain't no doubt he done it."

"Was Jack with you?" Vincent asked, hoping that Turley would tell him that the deputy was at the preacher's house breaking the bad news.

"He's standin' guard with the prisoner and the body, waitin' for you to come out there. He said you'd have to be the one to go and tell the preacher."

Vincent had been afraid of that. He sighed and got off the desk. There was no use putting it off.

On the other hand, maybe he should go out to the scene and see if Turley was right in saying that Lizzie Randall was dead. There was always a chance that he was wrong, and it wouldn't be right to give the Randalls a false report, only to find out that there had been some kind of mistake. Maybe the girl was just badly beaten.

"Where'd you say she was?" he asked.

"Didn't say. But she's out in that grove of trees over to the west of town."

"Let's go," Vincent said.

"Ain't you gonna wait for the doc?"

"He's here," Vincent said, and then Turley,

too, heard the sound of a buggy driving up outside the jail.

They went out where Doc Bigby and Lane Harper were waiting, Harper on horseback and Bigby in the buggy. Bigby was the most cheerful man in Dry Springs. Vincent had never seen him without a smile or a chipper remark to make.

"Howdy there, Sheriff," Bigby sang out as the two men came out of the jail. "You ever see such a fine night at this time of the year? I swear, the air's like ambrosia." Bigby took a deep breath, and Vincent could see his teeth shining in the starlight.

Bigby was a short, dapper man, with a fringe of white hair showing under the brim of his hat. It was just about all the hair he had. Vincent liked the man in spite of his constant good cheer. Vincent couldn't quite figure out how anybody could be that happy all the time.

It wasn't his practice, that was for sure. Most of the people in Dry Springs knew that Bigby wasn't a real doctor, and though he seemed to know a little something about most ailments, they would often just as soon trust their own remedies as call on him.

Whenever there was a real emergency, however, or whenever somebody needed a tooth pulled or an extra pair of hands, or even whenever there was a really sick horse or cow that just didn't seem to be getting any better, Bigby was the man they looked for. Sometimes his cures worked, and sometimes they didn't, but he did well enough to keep from scaring everyone completely away. Besides, he was the closest thing Dry Springs had to a doctor, and the closest they were likely to get. And at least he wasn't overly fond of cutting off your body parts, like some doctors Vincent had run into over the years.

He looked a little less than dapper this evening, and when Vincent asked, he explained that a horse had foaled out at the Stuart place and there'd been a pretty rough time of it.

"But I understand you folks got you a real problem," Bigby said, still smiling.

"That's right," Vincent told him. "If what I've heard is right, we got some trouble."

"Well, let's get on out there and see. You might's well ride with me, Sheriff. I could use the company, and you could tell me what's goin' on."

Vincent tied his horse to the back of the buggy and climbed in, making the springs squeak.

"Could use some grease, I guess," Bigby said. His teeth flashed.

"You fellas go on ahead," Vincent told Turley and Harper. "We'll follow along after you."

The horses walked around the buggy and the two men started for the west side of town. Bigby slapped the reins on the neck of his little bay, and the buggy moved off after them.

"Harper says that Lizzie Randall's been murdered in cold blood," Bigby said as the buggy rolled along.

"That's what Turley tells me," Vincent said. "I was hopin' maybe they were wrong about that."

"About her bein' murdered?"

"About her being dead. They ain't experts."

Bigby looked sideways at the sheriff. "From what Harper said, there's not much doubt."

"We'll check it out anyway."

"I could tell the family for you," Bigby said. "I've had to do that kind of thing before."

Vincent was sorry he was that easy to read. "I'll do it. It's my job. I just want you to make sure."

"I understand they've got the fella that did it, too," Bigby said.

"Paco Morales. I ain't too sure about that, either."

"Why not?"

"Turley's story didn't exactly fit together real smooth."

"Harper says the Morales boy did it. Says they caught him in the act."

"That's what Turley says, all right. But he

didn't know how the girl died, or *if* she died. So how did they catch him in the act and not know that?"

"I see what you mean." Bigby thought about it for a minute. "This could get bad, Sheriff. If she's really dead, and if that Meskin kid was really there."

"He was there, all right. They caught him."

"Lots of folks won't like that, a Meskin kid around where a white woman's been killed. 'Specially a preacher's daughter. Lane Harper says they shoulda hung the boy right there. Would've done it if Jack Simkins hadn't stopped them."

"Jack stopped them?"

"That's what Harper says."

"I'll be damned." Vincent wouldn't have thought Jack had the nerve to stand up to a bunch that wanted to hang somebody. Maybe there was more to Jack than he thought.

"We're comin' to the trees," Bigby said.

Vincent didn't answer. He was afraid of what they'd find.

Chapter Six

She was dead, all right. Vincent knew that the minute he saw her, the light of the moon falling on her through the trees. He shook his head. "Have a look at her, Doc," he said.

"I tell you, I never seen anything like it," Harl Case said. "That damn Paco."

"Where is he?" Vincent said.

Harl hitched a thumb over his shoulder. "Back yonder in the trees."

Leaving the examination of the body to Bigby, Vincent walked back there, his boots scuffing through dried leaves. He saw Jack leaning against the tree. "Well, Jack."

"Yeah," Jack said. He looked like some kind of vengeful ghost standing there, his glass eye not quite lined up right, the scar on his face livid in the dim light.

Vincent looked down at Paco. "Jesus, they did a real job on him. He still alive?"

"I think so. I checked a few minutes ago, and he was still breathin' then."

"Better get him back to the jail and lock

him up, then. You think we can carry him?"

Simkins pushed away from the tree. "He don't weigh that much."

"Let's try not to hurt him any more than he already is," Vincent said as they bent down. They took the unconscious boy by his legs and shoulders and lifted him.

Paco groaned, and a bubble of blood formed on his mouth.

"Broke ribs," Vincent said. "We'll have to get Doc Bigby to look at him." He looked at Simkins. "You did good, Jack, not lettin' those fellas hang him."

"They might try it again. They were mad as hell."

They carried the injured boy to Bigby's buggy and laid him in the seat. Vincent was aware of the men watching them from the edge of the trees.

Bigby walked over. "Looks like she was beat up on pretty good, knifed a few times. I'll have to look her over better to know for sure."

"All right. Let's put her in the back of the buggy. You can take her to your office."

Bigby had a little office and examination room over the store where Paco had gone to buy the salt and sugar.

"There's some of us don't like the idea of her bein' in the buggy with that greaser,"

Turley Ross said when Vincent told the men what he was going to do.

"That's just too damn bad," the sheriff said. "There's not much he can do to her now."

"It don't seem right," Harl said. "Seein' as how he's the one killed her."

"I don't want to hear any more of that kind of talk," Vincent said. "Not until it's proved."

"It's proved enough for me," Ross said. "I say we hang the bastard right now."

"You all tried that idea out once already," Jack said. "It didn't wash, and it still won't. Go on home now. Get some sleep."

The men grumbled for a few more minutes, but finally they gave it up. They went over to where their horses were tied to some low-hanging branches, mounted up, and rode away.

"I think we'll be hearin' some more from them," Jack said.

"I'm afraid you're right," Vincent said. "Doc, you go on into town. I'll ride along with Jack, and you can meet us at the jail. In the mornin' we'll see what you can tell us about the girl."

He watched Bigby climb wearily into the buggy and thought about what he was going to tell the Randalls. Whatever he said, it would not be easy.

Chapter Seven

It turned out to be worse than he thought.

The Randalls' house was on the outskirts of town. It had a neatly kept yard surrounded by a picket fence, and someone, probably Mrs. Randall, had tried to start a flower garden. It had not done well, and Vincent could see only a couple of droopy-headed roses on a scraggly bush.

Martha Randall let him in the door at his knock, leading him to the lamplit sitting room. There was a hooked rug on the floor, and Vincent looked at its pattern as if there might be a message there for him.

There wasn't, and he took off his hat, bringing his head up, and met Mrs. Randall's eyes. "Where's your husband?" he asked.

"He's in the back room praying. Have you found my daughter? Have you found Lizzie?"

"We'd better get your husband in here," Vincent said, knowing it was the wrong thing but unable to think of anything better.

Mrs. Randall looked at him stonily, then

turned and left the room, her broad back tensed as if she expected Vincent to hit her.

In a few seconds Randall entered the room, clutching his Bible. His wife stood behind him in the doorway, filling it.

"You've found her?" Randall said. "Where is she?"

"Yes," Vincent said, twisting his hat in his hands. "We've found her. She . . . she's at Doc Bigby's office."

"She's hurt? What happened? A fall? Did she —"

"She's dead," Vincent blurted out. He couldn't think of any other way to put it. Hell, there wasn't any other way.

Mrs. Randall gave a brief, strangled cry and fell forward. She hit the floor hard, and Vincent was glad for the momentary distraction. He stepped past Randall and knelt down beside her. There was a horsehair sofa on one side of the room, and it had been his intent to get her to it, but he saw that he could not do so without help.

He got her rolled over onto her back, and then he felt Randall's heavy hand on his shoulder. "Leave her. Tell me what happened to my daughter."

Vincent stood up slowly. His knees popped. Maybe it was better this way. Mrs. Randall wouldn't have to hear the terrible details, at least not from the sheriff.

Randall stood stiffly while Vincent told him.

"There must be some mistake," he said when the sheriff had finished. "My daughter can't have been killed like that."

There was a faint stirring from Mrs. Randall, and what might have been a sigh. Vincent looked down at her, but she gave no sign of being aware of anything. Her eyes were closed.

"It's her," Vincent said. "There's no mistake."

Randall walked over to the sofa and sat down. He put his Bible down carefully on an end table covered with a white crocheted doily. Then he clasped his hands and bowed his head.

Vincent stood there awkwardly. He didn't know whether to stay or go, but he felt he should do something for Mrs. Randall if her husband didn't intend to.

She lay on the floor unmoving, however, and Randall continued to pray silently. Or Vincent guessed he was praying. That was what it looked like he was doing.

"She's at the doc's, like I said," Vincent said finally, but Randall ignored him, and his wife did not hear.

Nothing changed for a full five minutes, so Vincent walked to the front door and let himself out.

There was another house he had to visit that night.

The home of Paco Morales was quite different from that of the Randalls. There was no fence, and no flower garden, not even the pretense of one. Even in the moonlight, Vincent could see that the roof needed repair and the paint was peeling. The yard was hard dirt, and there were some chickens roosting in the lower limbs of a chinaberry tree near the house.

There was a light in one of the front windows, and it occurred to Vincent for the first time that there was another mother who had most likely been up all night waiting for her child to come home.

He knocked on the door, and it was answered immediately by a short, round-faced woman with coal-black hair and anxious eyes.

"Miz Morales?" Vincent said. He knew very well who she was. He had met her more than once when her husband had been killed.

"*Sí*, I am Consuela Morales, Sheriff."

"It's, uh, about your son."

"Paco. Where is Paco?" The voice came from a little girl about six years old who was standing beside Mrs. Morales. Vincent hadn't noticed her earlier.

"Go to the bedroom, Aurelia," Mrs. Morales said. "It is time that you were asleep."

"But where is Paco?"

"Never mind about that. Go to bed." The woman's voice was firm, and the little girl turned reluctantly away.

Her mother watched her go. When the girl was gone, Mrs. Morales turned back to Vincent. "And now, as my daughter asked, where is Paco? Where is my son?"

"Well, ma'am, he's in the jail."

The anxiety in Mrs. Morales's voice changed to something else. "Why is he in the jail?"

"He killed —" Vincent caught himself. "He might have killed a girl tonight. I ain't sure."

Mrs. Morales seemed to shrink a little somehow. It was probably just that her shoulders sagged, but it seemed to Vincent that she actually grew smaller.

"Killed a girl? Paco would never kill anyone. I sent him to the store for salt and sugar, and he has not returned. But he would not kill anyone."

Vincent felt immensely uncomfortable. He had the feeling that he had heard all this before, three years ago, when her husband had been killed. She couldn't believe he had cheated anyone, either.

"Maybe he didn't kill anyone," Vincent said. "But it looks bad for him. He was caught pretty close to the body."

"And who was this person Paco is supposed to have killed?"

"Lizzie Randall. The preacher's daughter."

Mrs. Morales did it again, shrank up even smaller in the doorway. "Miss Randall," she said.

"You know her?" Vincent said, surprised.

"No," Mrs. Morales said quickly, too quickly it seemed to the sheriff. "I did not know her. And Paco did not kill her."

"Well, it'll be up to the judge and jury to decide that," Vincent said.

"Paco, he is all right? He is safe in the jail?"

Vincent decided to answer the second question. "He's safe. I won't let anything happen to him."

"I can see him? Now?"

Vincent didn't think that would be a good idea. "Better wait till mornin'. You can come in then."

Maybe Bigby would have looked the boy over by that time, cleaned him up. Even if Paco was a killer, his mother shouldn't have to see him looking the way he did now.

"I will be there in the morning, then. Paco killed no one, Sheriff. Whoever says he did is a liar."

And with that she closed the door in Vincent's face.

Chapter Eight

The jail was hot and still, and Paco Morales lay sweating on the cot in one of the tiny cells. Luckily, he was still not conscious. Doc Bigby was cheerfully putting the boy's broken arm in a sling, having already bound his ribs.

"What do you think, Doc?" Vincent asked.

"He'll live," Bigby said. "They must've beat the hell out of him, though."

"What about the girl?"

"Haven't had time to look at her yet. Got to get to it, though. In this heat . . ."

He didn't need to finish the sentence.

When he had left, Vincent sent Jack on home. The night was almost over anyhow, and the sheriff had decided that he might as well be the one to sit it out. He wanted to be there when Paco Morales woke up so he could ask him a few questions.

Paco woke in a haze of pain. There wasn't a part of his body that didn't hurt, and for a moment he thought that he must still be in the grove, still taking the kicks being dealt out to him by the men.

After a while he knew that he was not lying on the ground but on something softer, though not much softer. He opened his eyes, and even that was painful. He tried to raise his hand to his face, but he found that he could not.

It was too dark to see much, but he could tell that he was in some kind of small room. There was a square of lighter darkness above him which he assumed was a window.

A door opened at the end of a hall somewhere.

"You awake, boy?"

"Yes," Paco croaked. "I am awake." His throat was dry and very sore. Someone had kicked him even in the throat.

He heard footsteps and then the sound of a key in a lock. There was a squeak of a door opening very near him.

"I'm the sheriff," a voice near him said. "Can you sit up?"

Paco tried, but he could not raise himself. The pain was too much.

He felt a hand go under his head and lift it.

"Try to drink some of this water." A dipper was pressed to his parched lips.

Paco managed to take a few sips. The water

felt cold and sweet as it trickled down his throat.

"Where am I?" he said.

"In the jail. Looks like you're in a little trouble, boy."

"The men, they beat me. They —"

"I know about that. Question is, what did you do?"

"Nothing. I did nothing. I was going home from the store, and I found the woman. . . ." The sentence ended with a soft groan of pain. Vincent did not know whether Paco was groaning because he was hurt or because of the woman.

"Found her, huh? You didn't have anything to do with her bein' there in the first place?"

"No! No! I bought some salt and sugar at the store, and then I talked to Juanito García. When I was going home, I found her in the trees."

"What did you kill her with, son?"

"I did not kill her! I found her there!"

Vincent thought about it. There was the sound of truth in the boy's voice, and his mother said something about the salt and sugar.

"Where's the sugar and salt, then?" he asked.

Paco could not remember. "I . . . I lost it. I was afraid when I found her, and I ran."

Well, that was possible. But it was possible that he lost it when he attacked the girl, too. Vincent would have to go give the place the once over when it got light. There was more than the salt and sugar worrying him. If Paco had killed the girl, maybe stabbed her, the doc said, what had he done it with? Paco didn't have a knife, and there hadn't been one lying in the trees, not that Vincent could see. He'd have to have a talk with Juanito García, too.

Vincent gave Paco another sip of the water. "You try to rest, son. I've told your mother that you're here. She'll probably come in to see you. You'll be all right."

With that, he left the cell. Paco, trying not to twist with the pain, fought his fear as he lay on the cot and thought about being all right. He knew by now that there was something very wrong with his ribs and that his arm was most certainly broken, since it was caught up in some kind of sling.

He was pretty sure that he would never be all right again.

Sheriff Vincent put the worn heels of his boots up on the desk top and leaned back in the old wooden chair, balancing it delicately on two legs. It was still a long time to daylight, but he wasn't going to be able to sleep. His stomach was churning around, and all kinds of thoughts were spinning in his head.

He thought about the Randalls and the way they'd acted, or the way the preacher had acted, mostly. Leaving his wife just lying there like that. Vincent had never see anything quite like it.

And Mrs. Morales and her quiet assurance that her son had not done anything. It seemed like that family was doomed to trouble. First the father, now the son.

But what worried him most was that he believed Paco and his mother. He was almost convinced that the boy was innocent.

And what was wrong with that? he thought.

Nothing, except that there were four or five others who were equally sure Paco was guilty and who were spoiling for trouble, the kind of trouble that Vincent had done his best to avoid, the kind of trouble that could get people killed.

He swung his legs off the desk, and the chair hit the wood floor with a thump. He would just have to mosey on over to Bigby's and see what the doc had found out about the way the girl had died. He hated to leave his prisoner, but he figured that the boy would be safe that night. If anyone got worked up enough for a necktie party, it wouldn't be until later. At least he hoped so.

Meantime, maybe Bigby could tell him

something. Like that it had all been a mistake and the girl died in a fall.

He locked the front door of the jail as he left.

Chapter Nine

Hank Moran had drifted into Sharpsville a couple of days before, not on his way to anywhere in particular, just looking for a place to hang his hat and play cards for a day or two. Sharpsville was close to a place called Dry Springs, a place where he'd had a spot of bad luck a few years back, but that didn't bother him. He was superstitious about a lot of things, but not about killing a Mexican.

There were only three other men left in the saloon, the bartender and the two men at Moran's table. The bartender was ready to close the place up, and he stood behind his long bar, polishing and repolishing it with a greasy rag.

The other two were not as eager to leave. There was a pile of their money in front of Moran, and they wanted to get it back. It seemed to both of them that something was slightly wrong with the way the game was going, but neither could figure out just exactly what it might be.

There had been others in the game earlier, but they had all cut their losses and left at a decent hour. Before too long the roosters would be crowing and it would be time to go to work.

Moran was cheerfully dealing one more hand. He was a thin, pale man with cadaverous cheeks, and he looked like a smiling corpse. He carefully avoided what he thought to be a common failing of some other gamblers he knew, taking great care never to appear too flashy. He wore faded Levi's, a white cotton shirt, a tan vest, and suspenders.

Strapped to his leg was the .44 that had killed Roberto Morales. That had been an unfortunate event brought about by Morales's catching on to Moran's habit of marking the cards, something that no one else had ever done, before or since, though of course he had often been accused of cheating and had been involved in more than one powerful dust-up, the kind of thing that he regarded as merely an occupational hazard.

Moran was not greedy, however, and he did not like to take risks. To keep his troubles to a minimum, he never resorted to fancy devices like holdouts or shiners. He never dealt from the bottom or got fancy with cutting the deck, and he never tried to ring in a cold deck. In fact, he never offered to provide the cards for

65

any game. He always had a fresh deck or two on him, but he used them only when asked.

What he did was simple. He marked the deck he was using, whoever it belonged to, during the course of the game.

His hands were long and soft, his fingers supple and quick, his fingernails sharp, especially the nail of his right thumb, which was filed to razor keenness. All it took was a nick on the edge of the important cards — the aces, a few of the faces — to give Moran all the advantage he needed. The nick was so small as to be undetectable to any cursory examination, or even to a fairly careful one, but it was easily recognized by Moran's talented fingers.

It was not the kind of trick that would go unnoticed for very long by any sophisticated gambler, not the kind of thing that Moran could get away with for very long in a town of any size, but it worked like a charm as long as he limited himself to small-stakes games in small towns, or it had except for the one incident that Moran would just as soon have forgotten.

How the Mex had ever figured out that the cards were nicked was something Moran had not been able to guess. The Mex's hands had been work hardened and callused, the kind of hands Moran liked to see in a game, and it just didn't seem possible that he had been able to feel the slight cuts in the cards.

He didn't regret killing the man; he had been forced into it. But he did regret the fact that his activities had been limited for a good while afterward. Word got out, and people were suspicious.

All that was behind him now, though, and he was having an easy time of it, taking money from folks in backwaters like Sharpsville and drifting along as he pleased.

He had just about worn out his welcome here, he reckoned as he dealt the hand. Time to move on down the road, maybe pay another call on Dry Springs. Probably there was hardly anyone there who even remembered his last visit.

First he had to get through this hand, however. The two men held their cards close, looking them over.

One of them, a farmer by the look of him, glowered at Moran over the rim of the cards. His flat-topped straw hat with its broad black band sat squarely on the middle of his square head, and his jaw jutted out defiantly.

The other, the town dandy, Moran guessed, wore a tie and a gray suit. He had sweated through his shirt, and Moran was sure that he had lost more than he could afford. So had the farmer, for that matter. Otherwise they would have quit long ago instead of trying to win it back.

Neither of the men had a very good hand as far as Moran could tell. No more than one face card each. He, on the other hand, was holding a couple of aces and a king.

The farmer bet two dollars, and the dandy matched him. Moran tossed in two as well.

"Three cards," the farmer said sullenly. Moran slid them across the table with a smile.

"Three for me, too," the dandy said, and Moran cheerfully supplied them, especially since his educated thumb told him that an ace was the next card.

He decided to take only two cards, and getting the second king along with the ace was pure luck. He appreciated that, being an admirer of luck in any form.

"Five dollars," the farmer said. It was all he had left.

The dandy went along reluctantly.

"Since that seems to be about all you gentlemen have on you tonight, I'll call," Moran said.

The farmer put down three eights; the dandy had two pair. Moran's full house beat them easily.

The farmer's face turned brick red. "You son-of-a-bitch cheater," he said.

The dandy reached out and put a hand on

his friend's tensed arm. "Now, Joe, we don't know —"

"Don't you tell me 'bout what I know. That son of a bitch is cheatin', and I'm gonna make him give me my money back."

Moran retained his smile. Under cover of the table, his hand slipped to the smooth butt of the .44. "I don't return money that I've won fair and square, gentlemen."

The farmer was not satisfied. "Fair and square, my ass. I don't know how you done it, but you done it. That's for sure."

Moran shoved the table against the farmer's chest, making it difficult for the man to get out of the chair with any speed. "I'm sorry that you feel that way," he said. "Maybe you'd better go on home now."

"He's right," the dandy said. "We'd better go on home."

The farmer shook off his friend's hand. "All right, we'll go. But the son of a bitch is still a cheater."

They pushed back their chairs and stood up.

Moran kept his hand on the handle of the pistol in his lap until they had left the saloon. Then he holstered the gun and gathered in his winnings.

He walked over to the bar and had one last drink, then stepped through the batwings. The full moon was sinking low in the sky, but it silvered the silent buildings and the dirt of the street.

Moran did not pause to admire the view. He moved down the board-walk, his boot heels striking hollowly and the sound echoing off the walls. There was no one else in sight.

He stepped off the walk at the end of the block, and that was when they got him, coming at him out of the alley in a rush, their fists swinging before he had a chance to react.

It was the dandy and the farmer, and they had been both smarter than he had given them credit for and more bitter than he had thought. They had left, but they had not given up on getting their money back.

One of them hit him in the face and he reached out, grabbing a handful of shirt that ripped as he went down. He rolled over, avoiding a kick, and swung out his legs, tangling them with the legs of the dandy and causing him to fall heavily.

He drew his .44, but the farmer kicked it out of his hand. It landed somewhere in the dark of the alley.

Moran got to his feet, dodged a blow, and hammered his fist into the farmer's chest, directly over his heart.

The farmer staggered back into the wall of the nearest building, sucking for breath, his eyes bugging out and his mouth working like that of a fish thrown on the bank of a river.

Moran moved in on the man, smashing him again and again in the chest and stomach. If the wall had not been holding him up, the farmer would have collapsed to the ground.

He did fall when the dandy jumped on Moran's back, dragging the gambler backward.

Moran kept going back until he hit the building on the other side of the alley, or, rather, the dandy hit it. All the breath went out of him, and he dropped off Moran's back.

He tried to get up, but Moran kicked him under the chin. The dandy's teeth slapped together with a loud click, and his eyes rolled up in his head.

Goddamn sore losers, Moran thought as he was going through their pockets to see if there was any money in there that he hadn't already taken from them.

There wasn't, which was just as well. He wasn't really a thief, and he had never robbed anyone before, at least not unless they had been sitting at a poker table together, and that didn't really count in Moran's book. Any man who got into a game of chance was fair game. If he let himself be taken, that was too damn bad.

He wasn't fond of trouble, and it was time

that he was leaving Sharpsville anyway. These two wouldn't have anything good to say about him when they woke up, and it was for sure they wouldn't tell anyone the truth of the matter. Most likely they would lie and say that he had been the one who attacked them and took all their money. It would be easier for them to admit that than to say they had lost it all gambling.

He'd just go over to the livery and get his horse, then head on down the road. It was late, but that didn't make much difference. He'd gone without sleep before.

He'd move on down to Dry Springs, trim a few suckers, and maybe ride down into Mexico for a spell. He'd heard the Mexicans were big gamblers, and it was high time he found out for himself.

He whistled tunelessly as he walked on down the street, not looking back to the two who lay in the alley.

He had forgotten them already.

Chapter Ten

The sun woke Willie Turner, shining under the brim of his hat and hitting him right in the eyes.

It had been doing that a lot more lately, and he was a little worried about it. A man of his age ought not to be sleeping outside all night without even a blanket. Wasn't good for the bones.

It took Willie a while to get accustomed to the light and to get his eyes open, but when he did he looked around him. He was behind Danton's Saloon, sort of leaned up against the wall. There was a rain barrel propping him up on one side, and he could see the outhouse a few yards away, not far from the shacks where one or two of the saloon girls lived, the ones Danton didn't allow to have rooms upstairs.

Willie closed his eyes again. The sun was giving him a terrible headache on top of the one he already had. He felt like there was a bucking bronco inside his head, kicking him right behind the eyes, and he wondered just how much he'd had to drink the night before.

It scared him a little that he couldn't remember.

It was getting to be that way more and more. He'd wake up somewhere, and he couldn't remember how he got there or where he'd been before he got there.

He thought about it for a few minutes, his shoulder rubbing on the barrel, but it didn't do any good. He was there, but that was it. How much he'd drunk or where he'd been the night before were as blank as the blue sky that hung over Dry Springs.

Something almost came to him then, something that made his head slump suddenly forward and his knees jerk up as if he were going to jump up and run.

Something had happened last night, something bad. Really bad.

Willie hugged himself tightly, as if he were cold, and rocked gently back and forth, moaning.

After a minute or two, however, he composed himself. What was there to be scared of? Something had happened, and it had been awful, but he could not for the life of him recall what it had been. What was wrong with him? Why couldn't he remember?

He sat a little straighter and pulled his hat

brim down so the sun didn't bother him quite so much.

Hell, why should he worry about not being able to remember? That was why he'd taken up drinking in the first place, wasn't it? So as not to remember?

Trouble was, he could remember all the things he didn't want to. He could remember Laura Lee just fine, see her face shining and smiling, and see her brown hair hanging around it. He could see their baby, too, a little girl, it was. Laughing and taking on, grabbing at her daddy's finger.

That was the way they'd been before the fever took 'em, and the only blessing in Willie's life was that he could remember them that way and not as they had been in the last days of the fever, just before they'd died.

What was it the preacher had said? Randall, that was his name. "Ashes to ashes, dust to dust"? Something like that. And something about the sun also arising and going down and generations passing away, not one bit of which made a damn bit of difference to Willie.

If it was meant as a comfort, it missed the mark by a long sight, and since that time the only comfort Willie had found was in a bottle.

He could afford it. He'd sold his little farm and was determined to drink up the proceeds. He figured he'd be able to drink himself to death before he ran out of money, and he hoped he could. He was too much of a coward to shoot himself, though it would have been a good bit quicker and probably cleaner in the long run.

Clean was one thing that Willie was not. He couldn't recall his last bath, but he had slept out in the rain a time or two and so he figured that counted as a wash.

He hadn't changed clothes in quite a spell, either, and he knew he smelled to high heaven. Well, it didn't bother him, and to hell with anyone it did.

Using the wall, he pushed himself up.

He knew exactly what he needed. He needed a drink.

He moved away from the wall. His first step was somewhat unsteady, but by the time he had gone four or five steps he was getting the hang of it and was walking almost normally. He entered the alley beside the saloon, appreciating the cool shade it offered. Feeling a wave of dizziness, he rested for a minute, steadying himself with a hand on the wall.

After a while the dizziness passed and he went on down the alley. When he got to the end, he shaded his eyes with his hand. The street was not busy yet, but there were several wagons moving and some horses were tied to the hitching post in front of Danton's Saloon. They stood there calmly, twitching their sides when flies landed on them.

He stepped up on the walk and entered the saloon. There was hardly anyone in there at this hour. Lane Harper was behind the bar, and several men were leaning on it, talking to Harper in low voices.

Aside from them, there was no one. Roscoe, the piano player, would not be in until late afternoon, and few of the girls would be around before that time. Willie didn't care. He wasn't interested in music or women. All he wanted was a drink.

He walked over to the bar. The conversation, which had been hushed to begin with, stopped altogether when he got there.

He didn't give a damn. He reached into the pocket of his ragged Levi's and came up with a coin.

"Whiskey," he said, putting the coin on the bar.

"Early, ain't it?" Harper said. "Even for you."

Willie didn't say anything. Talking made his head hurt. He just waited, and Harper poured him a shot in a grimy glass, took the coin, and left Willie's change on the bar.

Willie knocked the drink back. He felt better almost at once. He knew the feeling would not last; it never did. But it was enough to get him going for the day.

He looked down the bar. Turley Ross was there, and Len Hawkins. Harl Case, too. To Willie, they looked to be in bad shape. Their eyes were as red as his probably were, and they were all scowling. Come to think of it, Harper didn't look so good himself.

"You fellas look like you could use a drink," Willie told them.

"Just go on off and leave us alone," Ross said.

"Don't think so," Willie said. "Gimme another one, Lane."

Harper poured another drink. Willie took his time with this one, waiting to see if the men would resume their conversation.

Finally they did.

"Be a damn shame if he got away with it," Ross said. "You never know what can happen in a trial."

"You think we oughta do somethin' ourselves?" Harper said.

"It ain't the time to be thinkin' of that," Harl Case said. "He's in the jail now. We got to let the law handle it."

"Handle what?" Willie said.

Ross gave him a speculative look, as if wondering whether to tell him. "Paco Morales," he said. "He killed a woman last night."

"Paco did? I can't hardly believe that," Willie said. "He's just a kid."

"Well, he killed her just the same," Len Hawkins said, running a hand over his bald head. "We seen it."

"Who'd he kill?"

"That preacher's daughter, Lizzie Randall."

Willie Turner's stomach contracted itself into a knot and he doubled over at the bar, dropping his empty glass and clutching at himself.

"Son of a bitch is gonna puke," Harper said. "Get him outa here before he does it."

Turner was already coughing from deep within himself. Turley Ross, who was closest to him, got him turned around and headed in the direction of the door. Then he planted his foot in the middle of Willie's backside and pushed.

Willie went stumbling out the door, across the boardwalk, and into the middle of the street. He stood there hunched over and retched, bringing up a thin green bile along with the whiskey he had just drunk. It splattered into the dust of the street and on Willie's boots. It could have been worse, but Willie could not recall the last time he'd had a real meal.

There was still hardly anyone on the street, and no one noticed Willie as he stood there heaving, bent over with his hands braced on his knees.

Paco Morales had killed Lizzie Randall, he thought. That wasn't right. He was sure it wasn't right.

He staggered back into the alley, into the shade.

Lizzie Randall. That was the bad thing that had happened. He could see the blood. It was all over her. He leaned a shoulder against the wall and heaved again, but nothing came up.

Lizzie Randall. Jesus, he was scared.

He had to have a drink. No, not a drink. That wasn't what he needed right now. What he needed was a bottle. A full bottle.

Maybe two.

Chapter Eleven

"She wasn't stabbed," Bigby had told Vincent when the sheriff had arrived at the doctor's office. "Just cut real bad — slashed, you might say. That's why there was so much blood. What killed her was the beatin'." He wasn't smiling as much as he usually did.

Vincent found it hard to believe that there was anyone in Dry Springs who could do a thing like that, and he said so to Bigby.

"Anybody can do anything," Bigby said, shaking his head. "You put them in the right place at the right time, they can do anything."

"Where's the body now?"

"I called Rankin. He came and got it."

Rankin was the undertaker.

"Think he can do anything with her?" Vincent said.

"You mean make her look better? Maybe a little." Bigby didn't sound as if he held out much hope.

"The Randalls might be comin' by here. You send 'em on to Rankin's," Vincent said.

"They took it pretty hard, I guess."

"They did," Vincent said. "They surely did." He was thinking about the Randalls as he left Bigby's office.

He was in the grove now, looking for something, anything, that would help him figure out what happened. For one thing, he wanted to find the knife, if it was still there, though he suspected the killer had taken it with him.

He found the spot where the struggle had occurred. There were some blood stains on the ground, a piece of Lizzie's dress, but that was all. He took the piece of dress and put it in his pocket.

He located the place where the horses had been tied last night and then walked along the trail looking for some sign of other horses. If he found none, he would look in the trees.

He soon found some droppings beside the trail. He broke them open. They were fresh, but the ground was too hard to offer any tracks, and though he looked for quite a while, he found nothing that was any help to him. The droppings proved that someone else had been along the trail, maybe around the time of the murder, but that was all. They didn't have to come from the killer's horse. Lots of people used that trail.

If Paco was telling the truth, of course, there had to have been someone else in the grove

82

last night. It looked as if there had been, but that wasn't necessarily going to help Paco, who hadn't seen anyone except the men who had beaten him.

He continued to look around, moving back into the trees to the place where Paco had been lying. Not too far away, Vincent found the twisted sacks of salt and sugar.

He put them in his pocket with the piece of Lizzie's dress.

They didn't prove anything either, except that Paco had been telling the truth when he said that he had been to the store. He could still have killed the girl.

Vincent was liking the whole thing less and less. There was going to be trouble over this, he could tell it, the kind of trouble he had spent years trying to avoid.

His stomach lurched. He told himself it was just that he hadn't eaten breakfast, but he knew better. He was afraid of what might happen.

The men who had found the body were convinced Paco was guilty. They were going to start talking around town, and things could turn ugly fast.

The sun was getting higher in the sky. It was going to be another hot day. Vincent found himself wishing for rain, thinking that heavy clouds and pouring water might calm things down or at least postpone any violence that might be coming. But there was no hope of rain.

He walked wearily back to his horse. Maybe he would have been more optimistic if he had been able to sleep the night before, but it was too late to worry about that. He swung himself into the saddle and rode back to the jail, where Jack Simkins was waiting.

"How's the boy?" Vincent asked when he had tied his horse to the rail.

"Not doin' so good," Jack said. "He's scared."

"Don't blame him much," Vincent said. "I'd be scared, too."

"You ain't gonna let 'em hang him, are you?" Simkins said.

Vincent walked past him and into the cramped office. He opened a desk drawer and put the sacks and the piece of dress inside. "I don't intend to let them," he said. "Maybe they won't try."

"They'll try, all right," Jack said. "We gotta stop 'em." His face was set in a determined expression that emphasized the strangeness of his features.

Vincent hardly noticed the glass eye and the scar anymore, having gotten used to them over the years, but there were no doubt some who still found Jack's appearance pretty unusual.

It wasn't something that the deputy liked to talk about, and although Vincent knew the whole story, he wasn't sure how many of the townspeople did. Jack was prone to tell different versions.

"Lost it one time while breakin' a bronc," he might say. Or he might tell about the time he got in a little squabble with a grizzly bear over which one of them was going to cross a creek on a narrow log.

Whichever version he told, Jack always said that he liked being a deputy. He was tired of his old life and looking for something a little less strenuous. Somehow he had drifted into Dry Springs about the time Vincent had become sheriff and had gotten himself hired on as the only deputy, another job he had showed little natural talent for. However, since there was rarely any call for extraordinary law-enforcement ability in Dry Springs, he had managed to hang on to the job.

Vincent was surprised that he was taking such an interest in Paco Morales. Jack was usually looking for ways to avoid doing anything rather than ways to prevent trouble.

"What's got into you, Jack?" he said. "You got some kind of a special interest in that boy?"

Jack took off his hat and wiped the sweat band with his dirty bandanna. He put the bandanna back in his pocket and settled the hat on his head.

"Nope," he said. "I just hate to see him get railroaded."

Vincent sat in the chair behind the desk. "I got to ask you somethin', Jack."

"What's that?"

"Did you beat on that boy along with the rest of them?"

Jack looked at the floor, remembering the previous night. Finally he looked up. "Nope," he said. "I didn't."

"That's good," Vincent said, relaxing a little.

"But I stood there and watched 'em," Jack said. "Sheriff, I coulda stopped 'em if I'd just pulled my gun on 'em, but I didn't do it. I let 'em beat that boy to within an inch of his life, and I just watched. There wasn't nothin' he could do against all those men, and I let 'em hit him like that."

"I'm not sure there was anything you could've done, Jack. You didn't let 'em hang him. Remember that."

Jack did not seem reassured. "You better talk to the boy," he said. "It might make him feel better."

Vincent got up and went back to the cells. Paco was still lying on the cot, staring at the ceiling.

"You feel like you could eat somethin'?" Vincent asked.

Paco shook his head.

"How about some water?"

"Yes," Paco said. "Water would be good."

Vincent brought the bucket and dipper. Paco sat up and drank thirstily.

"Look, Paco," Vincent said when the boy had finished drinking. "This looks pretty bad for you, but maybe we could do something about it. If you saw anybody there last night, anybody who could say you didn't kill the girl, you could get out of this. Or if you didn't kill her, maybe you saw who did."

"I didn't see anyone," Paco said wearily. He sounded like a man who had already given up all hope. "I thought I heard someone once, but I was scared. I ran."

"There's a lot of men in town who are sayin' they saw you do it," Vincent told him.

"Then they are liars."

"They wouldn't cotton to you callin' 'em that."

"It does not matter. They will kill me anyway, the way they killed my father."

"Your father was caught cheatin'," Vincent reminded him.

"He cheated no one," Paco said. "That is another lie. But they killed him anyway, the same way they will kill me. You did nothing for him, and you will do nothing for me."

Vincent sighed. He hated himself for thinking it, but he was afraid that Paco was probably right.

Vincent went back to the office. Jack had gone off to make the rounds of the town, and Vincent had just settled back into the chair and thrown his legs up on the desk when the shooting started.

Chapter Twelve

Charley Davis was standing in the middle of the street looking up at one of the hotel's second-floor windows, the one where the shots were coming from. He was yelling up at the blond woman who leaned out the window, holding a .44-caliber Colt with both of her small hands and trying to squint one eye as she sighted down the barrel.

"Dammit, Lucille!" the man yelled. "You gotta listen to me. There's no reason for you to —"

He was interrupted by the crack of a shot. Smoke seemed to puff from the pistol's cylinder, and there was a short spout of flame from its barrel. The bullet whacked out a hunk of the dry street, and Davis hopped backward.

Davis was a tall, sandy-haired cowboy, not that you could see much of his hair under the large, tall crowned hat he wore. He had thin legs encased in tight Levi's, and he was wearing a faded red shirt and a black vest. He felt silly, standing in the street and getting shot at, and he knew that he was making a fool of himself in front of the whole town.

"Lucille, you got to listen to me!" he yelled. There were two more shots from the second-floor window, and one of them almost clipped the front toe off Davis's left working boot. He tried to jump back, got his legs tangled, and fell on his butt in the street.

He looked around to see if there was anyone laughing at him. By God, there better not be. If there was, they were going to be sorry if Charley got his hands on them.

No one was laughing. Most of the people on the street had taken cover when the shooting started, either in Danton's Saloon, which was right across the street from the hotel, or in one of the nearby stores. There were a couple of kids behind a water trough, and Davis could hear them giggling, but that was all right. They were just kids.

Lucille Benteen looked down at Charley sitting there with his knees in the air, twisting his head around to look to see who was watching him; it was all she could do not to laugh herself. But she didn't; she wasn't going to laugh at Charley ever again, any more than she would ever believe a word that worthless wrangler said.

While he was sitting there trying to decide whether to get up or not, she had a chance to reload, and she thumbed the thick cartridges into the chambers of the .44 with a practiced hand. She wasn't going to kill Charley, but she could if she wanted to, and he damn well ought to know it. Before she was finished with him, he might wish she *had* killed him. She was going to embarrass the fire out of him, that was for sure.

Lucille Benteen was young, beautiful, and rich. Her father owned most of the land around Dry Springs, and what he didn't own he could afford to buy if he wanted it. She did not have to put up with the likes of Charley Davis trifling with her. She couldn't believe that she had ever listened to him in the first place. Maybe it was those pale blue eyes, or the way he put his head over to the side and looked at her when he talked to her. He had a smooth way with words, she had to give him that.

She slapped the cylinder back into place and leaned out the window. Charley was up again, and now he had his hat off, holding it in his hands.

"Lucille," he called, "I wish you'd just give me a chance to talk to you about this. Your daddy —"

A bullet plowed the street beside him, but this time he didn't move. He had figured out that she wasn't going to hurt him.

"You leave my daddy out of this," she said. "I'll handle my daddy, don't you worry." She pulled the trigger again, and the heavy pistol jumped in her hand.

She didn't want to talk about her father. It was her father that had got her into this, all right, and she wasn't going back to his house ever again, or at least not for a while. She had a little money of her own, and she could live in the hotel for a good while if she had to. She wasn't going to let her father marry her off to some two-timing cow waddy, even if the waddy did have those pretty blue eyes.

She was about to squeeze off another shot when she saw someone running down the street from the direction of the jail.

Ward Vincent, she thought. Well, he didn't have much gumption, in her opinion. He wouldn't do anything to stop her, and if he tried, she'd just tell him why she was shooting up the town in the first place. That would give him a surprise, and it would shame Charley.

That was just fine with her. She didn't care if Charley was shamed. Right now she didn't care if they strung him up. In fact, that might make her feel better.

She glanced down the street in the other direction and saw Jack Simkins coming, too. The sheriff and his ugly deputy. They didn't

92

have enough grit between the two of them to fill up a turkey's craw. They wouldn't do anything to her. She was Roger Benteen's daughter, and they'd think twice before they tried to stop her from doing anything she wanted to do.

She let another bullet fly in Charley's direction.

It cracked a clod of dirt and showered the toe of Charley's boot, but he didn't move. He could see Vincent, too, and he was already wondering what he would say to the sheriff. It all depended on Lucille, he guessed.

"What the hell's . . . goin' on here?" Vincent huffed. He wasn't used to running. He looked up at the window. "Lucille Benteen, is that you?"

Lucille didn't say anything. She didn't pull the gun back inside the hotel room, either.

Jack arrived on the scene about that time. He was even more puzzled than Vincent. He had his pistol drawn and ready, but he looked as if he was uncertain about what to do with it.

Vincent had recognized Charley by then. Davis was Roger Benteen's foreman, in charge of taking care of all the rancher's land and cattle. It was probably the best job in the whole area, and it commanded a certain amount of respect.

"Put your gun up, Jack," Vincent said. "Charley, you want to tell me what this is all about?"

Charley did not want to tell, at least not all. He knew that he was going to have to tell some of it, however.

"Aw, it's nothin', Sheriff. Lucille — Miss Benteen — and I, we've had us a little argument."

"Argument?" Vincent said. "Looks more like a damn war to me."

Davis put his hat back on and settled it on his head. When he was satisfied, he said, "We got engaged, did you know that?"

Vincent had heard about it. So had most people in town. It was hard for most of them to believe that old Roger Benteen was going to let his little girl marry up with an ordinary cowhand, but it looked like that was the case. In fact, the way Vincent heard the story, the old man was all in favor of the marriage.

"If you're engaged, why's she shootin' at you?" Jack asked. It just didn't seem right to him, a woman shootin' at a man. He couldn't remember ever seeing anything like that before.

It was a good question. Vincent looked up at the window and said, "Why're you shootin' at your intended, then, Miss Benteen?"

"Ask him," Lucille said. "He knows." She

pulled back the hammer of the pistol, and they could all hear the click it made when it locked into position.

Vincent took off his hat and wiped his forehead with a yellow bandanna handkerchief that he pulled from his back pocket. The run down the street had made him break out in a sweat all over, and he could feel his shirt sticking to his back. When he was finished wiping, he stuck the bandanna back in his pocket, but he didn't put the hat back on.

"Now then, Miss Benteen," he said reasonably, "you don't want to do any more shooting. Look at this street. Not a single person on it but us three men. You're scarin' all the people that need to be out and gettin' their day's work done."

Charley nodded in agreement. "He's right, Lucille. You and me, we just need to talk this over in private. We don't want to make a show out of our private business."

"What private business is that?" Jack said. He was still trying to figure out what was going on.

"It's nothin'," Davis said, trying to keep his voice low. He didn't want Lucille to hear.

She heard anyway. "Nothing! That's not what I'd call it, you low-lifed two-timer."

"Two-timer?" Jack said. "Are you two-timin' her, Charley? If you are, it's a real shame." He looked up at the beautiful young woman framed in the window. Why anybody would want to two-time a woman who looked like that was beyond him.

"He's a two-timer, all right," Lucille said. "I found out about it, and now he's trying to tell me that I've misjudged him. That's a good one. Misjudged him!" She laughed shortly. "I know what he is, and he's going to be sorry!"

She steadied the gun, getting ready to fire again, but Vincent called out and stopped her.

"Wait a second," he said. "Maybe all this is just a misunderstandin'. Let me talk to him."

"Fine. You do that. And then I'm going to finish him off."

"It's hot out here in the street," Jack complained. "Can't we talk about this somewhere else?"

"That might be a good idea," Vincent said. "But I don't think Miss Benteen's gonna go for it. Charley, what the hell have you got yourself into?"

Charley looked sheepish. "Nothin'," he said.

Vincent looked pointedly at the woman holding the gun on them. "That ain't nothin'."

"Well, not much more'n nothin', then," Charley said. "It's just that she found out I'd been seein' somebody else before I started to court her, and she got mad about it."

He looked up at the window. "But I swear I didn't see her again, Lucille. Not more'n once, anyway."

Lucille pulled the trigger. This time she shot a hole through the high crown of Charley's hat, which flew off his head and into the street.

"She ain't real happy with you, and that's a fact," Vincent said. "Who were you seein' anyway?"

"The preacher's daughter," Charley said. "Lizzie Randall."

"Uh-oh," Jack said.

And Vincent thought, Oh, hell.

Chapter Thirteen

Consuela Morales was determined that her son was not going to die for the killing of Elizabeth Randall, even if she had to tell what she knew. She had never told about the people she had helped before; that was one of the reasons why she continued to have people coming to her house. If she had told about their problems, then they would not have trusted her.

They had begun coming in the first place because many of them did not trust Dr. Bigby, or even if they trusted him, they did not think much of his abilities as a doctor. The truth was, many of her visitors had been to Bigby first and then, not being satisfied, had come to her.

She was never quite sure how she had received the reputation she had as a healer. It might have arisen because of the time she had cured one of the local men of the bite he had received from a rattler. She had happened to be nearby when he was bitten, and she had been able to cut the wound and suck out the poison. But she had done more. She had bound the wound and applied certain herbs that she knew about to the cut. It had healed perfectly and the man was convinced that she had saved him, not because of the cutting and the sucking of the poison, but because of the "secret" healing ingredients she had used.

He told others, and they came to her for one thing or another — minor illnesses, cuts that wouldn't heal, sprained ankles. She did what she could, and she was successful often enough to achieve the reputation of someone who knew the secrets of healing. Somehow that led to other things.

Like the women. The women came for two reasons, mainly. They came because they were unable to have children or because they were about to have a child that they did not want. She always refused to do anything for the latter cases; she believed along with her church that to kill the child in the womb was as great a sin as to kill anyone else.

Still they came, about one every year. Elizabeth Randall had been only one among them. Each hoped that Consuela might change her mind about helping her get rid of her child, and they all seemed convinced that she knew some arcane secret that would relieve them of the burden they so unwillingly carried.

She knew no such secret, but she tried to

help them in other ways, telling them to treasure the life they were bringing into being and encouraging them to help it grow strong and straight.

Most of them listened to her. Most.

Even Elizabeth Randall had seemed to listen, but there was a look in her eyes that seemed to indicate some defiance that still remained, a determination to look elsewhere for help.

She had looked in the wrong place, Consuela thought. Or maybe she had gone to the father of the child and demanded that he acknowledge her, that he do something to help. Maybe she had demanded that he marry her, though he might have been in no position to do so.

At any rate, all those things seemed to indicate to Consuela that her son was as innocent as she believed him to be. There might have been men — or one particular man — who had a reason to kill Elizabeth Randall, but her son was not that man.

She was going to make sure that everyone knew it, and she was going to begin by telling the Reverend Randall and his wife what she knew. She had not told the sheriff, but it was not yet the sheriff's business. And besides, she had no love for the sheriff. She believed that he had let her husband's killer go free. Nevertheless, she would tell him if she had to.

But first she would tell the girl's parents.

She did not go to the preacher's front door. She knew better than that. The Randalls might be Christians, but they would never have received someone of her standing at their front door.

Mrs. Randall answered her knock at the back and stood there looking blankly at her. It was as if she were staring at something just over Consuela's left shoulder. There was a bruise on her face as if someone had hit her there.

"May I come in, please?" Consuela said at last. "There is something that I must tell you."

"Oh," Mrs. Randall said. "What is it?" She did not seem very interested. It was obvious that her mind was on other things.

"I must tell it to both you and your husband," Consuela said.

Mrs. Randall absently opened the door and stepped aside. Consuela went past her and into the house.

"My husband is praying," Mrs. Randall said. "I don't think he wants anybody to bother him." She preceded Consuela into the living room, her bulk obstructing the other woman's view.

When they got into the other room, Martha Randall stood aside and Consuela could see that the reverend was indeed deep in prayer.

He was kneeling in front of the couch, his elbows resting on one of the cushions, his hands clasped and his head bowed. His eyes were tightly closed. His Bible was resting beside his right elbow. He seemed to be entirely motionless, like a statue clothed in black, but now and then there was a tic in his cheek that revealed that he was a living person.

Mrs. Randall said nothing. She simply stood there and stared at her husband's back.

Consuela wondered what to do. She did not want to intrude on the man's grief and his prayer, but she had to say what she had come to say. She had to let these people know that their daughter was pregnant with someone's child and that while Paco would have had no reason to want her dead, there might have been someone else who did.

She waited for several minutes before speaking. There was no sound in the room except for the buzzing of a fly that seemed to be trapped behind one of the curtains.

The air in the room was close and stifling. There were no open windows, and Consuela found it hard to breathe.

When she had waited as long as she could, she spoke. "*Señor* Randall, I have come to speak to you about my son, Paco Morales."

She might have been a mute for all the impression she made on Randall. He appeared to have heard nothing. Even his cheek stopped twitching.

"*Señor* Randall," she said again.

"He can't hear you," Mrs. Randall said. "When he's with the Lord like that, he can't hear a thing." Her voice was bitter. "If he could've heard some of the things I tried to tell him years ago, we might still have our daughter."

"It is your daughter I have come about," Consuela said.

Mrs. Randall looked at her then, as if realizing for the first time that there was really someone there.

"What about my daughter?" she said.

"They say my son — my Paco — that he killed her."

Mrs. Randall's face turned red, and Consuela felt a jolt of fear. Mrs. Randall was a formidable woman.

"Then what are you doing in my house?" Mrs. Randall demanded, clenching her hands into fists. "How dare you to come into my house and speak to me?" Her voice rose.

"Because Paco did not kill your daughter, *Señora*. My son would never do such a thing. It was done by someone with an evil reason, and my son had no such reason."

Some of the color drained from Mrs.

Randall's face. "What reason?" she said. "What do you mean?"

Consuela had wanted both Mrs. Randall and her husband to hear what she had to say, but the preacher had not looked up even at the loud tones the woman had used. Consuela decided that she would tell the woman.

By the time she had finished talking, Mrs. Randall was looking as much like a statue as her husband. She seemed to be hardly breathing, and she swayed on her feet like some gigantic boulder that might be about to tip over and start an avalanche.

"*Señora* Randall?" Consuela said. She was afraid that the woman might faint.

"Get out of here," Mrs. Randall said in a harsh whisper. "Get out of here and never come back." She looked anxiously at her husband.

"But *Señora,*" Consuela said, "I must tell your husband what I know. He must understand. . . ."

"He won't understand. He'll never understand. Just you get out of here. Get out before it's too late." Mrs. Randall interposed her body between her husband and Consuela and began to force Consuela backward, out of the room.

"But my son. Paco. They will kill him," Consuela said.

"That's better than havin' my husband kill *you,*" Mrs. Randall said, pushing at Consuela with her doughy hands. "Go on now. Get out of here."

Consuela got out.

When the back door slammed, the Reverend Randall opened his eyes, looked up, and took his Bible into his hand. Then he got slowly to his feet. His knees popped as he straightened to his full height.

He was watching the doorway as his wife came back into the room. As she entered, he opened his Bible and began to read in a resonant voice:

"'And the woman was arrayed in purple and scarlet color, and decked with gold and precious stones and pearls, having a golden cup in her hand full of abominations and filthiness of her fornication: and upon her forehead was a name written, Mystery, Babylon the Great, the Mother of Harlots and Abominations of the Earth.'"

"Don't," Martha Randall said. "Please. Don't."

"Harlot," Randall said. "The Mother of Harlots and Abominations of the Earth."

"No," Martha said. "No."

Randall's face was as somber as his voice. "The Great Whore of Babylon." He began to read again. "'And I saw the woman drunken with the blood of the saints, and with the blood of the martyrs of Jesus.'"

"She was your child," Martha said. "She was your daughter."

Randall continued to read. "'For her sins have reached unto heaven, and God hath remembered her iniquities.'" His voice rose in a frightening crescendo. "'Reward her even as she rewarded you, and double unto her double according to her works.'" He slammed the Bible shut with a slap that echoed from the walls in the hot, close room.

Martha Randall put her face into her hands and wept.

Chapter Fourteen

The wave of sickness that had passed over Willie Turner left him feeling weak and unhappy. He slunk back behind Danton's Saloon to sit in the shade and recover, though he was not sure he would ever get to feeling much better.

He was sure of one thing, however. He was sure that a bottle wouldn't help. It had seemed like a good idea at first, but he knew he would just keep right on drinking until he couldn't remember anything at all, and that wouldn't be of any help to anybody. Hell, the problem was that he couldn't remember much of what he wanted to recall, even though he was mostly sober.

He sat in the shade, his back to the saloon wall, his arms extended out and resting on his knees, his hands hanging down toward his ankles. Every now and then his stomach would knot up and threaten to make him puke again, but each time he managed to force the evil-tasting bile back down.

Elizabeth Randall was dead. That was what they had said in the saloon, and they were sure as to God right about that. Jesus, the blood! Some of those dark stains on his clothes — they were her blood!

He forced his mind away from that line of thinking and tried to concentrate on what else the men had said. Paco Morales. They said Paco had killed Liz. At first that hadn't seemed right to him, but the more he thought about it, the more it seemed that it could be true. Paco had something to do with it, all right. He could almost remember that much.

He thought about the blood again, and about how much of it there was. And about how it was on his clothes.

He couldn't tell anyone about that. If he did, why they might even think he had something to do with the killing, which of course he hadn't. Or anyway, he didn't think he had. He wouldn't want that bunch of fellas thinking he had, not the way they were talking in the saloon. They were pretty upset, sure enough, and it sounded like they were even thinking of doing something along the lines of lynching Paco Morales. Not that anybody had said exactly that, but it was clear they had it on their minds.

It was the same bunch, more or less, who had been in the saloon when Paco's daddy got killed by the gambler.

Willie had been in the saloon that day, too. It had happened not long after he had taken up serious drinking, and he could remember the sound of the gun, how loud it was in the room, and the way the Meskin had flown back out of the chair, the little spurt of blood from his chest, his boots kicking at the table, the way the chips had jumped in the air.

The rest of it wasn't clear in Willie's mind, not the way it ought to be in the mind of a man who could really remember things, but some of it was. That was something else he wasn't ever going to mention — what had happened in the saloon that day. It was something else he didn't even like to think about, not even the parts of it he could recall, so he turned his mind back to the night before. It seemed to him that this time he might ought to say something, but for the life of him he couldn't remember what it was he ought to say.

He could remember Liz, though, how she'd been when she was alive. A real sweet girl, and that was a fact, the kind who wasn't too good to talk to the town drunk like most folks would be if their daddy was the preacher.

Funny how he never really connected the two of them before, her and her daddy. He didn't like to think of the preacher. Randall. It made him think of the funeral of his wife and child, and he hated to think of that.

But the girl, she was different. She talked to him, told him her troubles, just like he was good as anybody else.

She'd sneak off to the grove to meet her sweethearts, and that was where Willie did some of his drinking. He didn't impose himself on her. He'd never do a thing like that, but sometimes if her sweetie was late and she knew he was around, she'd call him out and talk to him awhile.

He wished he could remember some of the fellas he'd seen there. Not Paco Morales, though. He'd never seen him. Who was it he'd seen? He wished his memory was better for things like that.

It improved right after the shooting started in the street. He got up, his curiosity aroused, and walked out to see what was going on, his knees threatening to give way at every step.

As soon as he saw Charley Davis, he knew who one of the fellas had been, the most recent one, in fact.

The knowledge did not make him feel any better. If anything, he felt worse, but he didn't know why. He had been right earlier. What he needed was a drink. He felt in his pocket to be sure that he had some money and went back into the saloon.

Harl Case and Len Hawkins were standing at the bar, though "standing" might not have been exactly the right word. It was more like they were leaning on it for support, their hands clasped around the glasses in front of them. Hawkins's smooth face was sagged down into a lugubrious frown, while Case was staring vaguely at his reflection in the mirror behind the bar.

Turley Ross had moved to a table where he had his own bottle, and Lane Harper had moved from behind the bar to join him. They were talking quietly about something when Willie entered.

Nobody seemed to notice him, so he tapped a coin on the bar to get their attention.

"We throwed you outa here once," Harper said. "You chip that bar, and you'll get worse than throwed."

"All I want's a drink," Willie said.

Harper got up reluctantly and moved back behind the bar. He poured the drink and took Willie's money.

Willie inhaled the whiskey. "You all see the shootin'?" he asked when he caught his breath.

"Yeah, we saw it," Turley Ross said from the table, his voice a little louder than it had to be. "We were hopin' somebody was shootin' that Meskin kid, but no such luck. What the hell was the trouble anyhow?"

"Don't know," Willie said. He asked Harper for another drink. "It might've had somethin' to do with the killin', I guess."

"You tellin' me that Lucille Benteen and Charley Davis are mixed up in this?" Hawkins said. "What do they have to do with it?" His voice was blurred by the whiskey he had been drinking.

"He used to court Liz — Charley did," Willie told them. He finished his second drink. "He wasn't the only one," he added vaguely.

"You tryin' to say somethin' about that girl's reputation?" Case demanded. "You want to be careful about that kinda thing. She's the preacher's daughter."

"I know who she is," Willie said. "Who she *was*, I mean. Don't make no difference, though. I know what I know."

Ross got up from his chair, picking up his bottle by the neck. He came over to the bar to stand beside Willie. "Just what the hell do you think you know?" He set his bottle down on the bar so hard it rattled Willie's glass.

Willie wished that he had kept his mouth shut. "Nothin'," he said. "Let me have another one, Lane."

"Not until you tell Turley what he wants to know," Harper said. "We're all real interested."

Willie didn't want to say anything. Liz Randall had treated him nice, and now they were asking him to say things he didn't want to say. But they were looking at him hard, and he wanted that drink.

"Sometimes she'd meet fellas in the woods," he said. "That's all."

"What fellas?" Ross said.

"Just fellas. I don't remember."

Ross grabbed Willie's shirtfront and twisted it in his fist. "Try," he said.

"I tried already," Willie said. "I can't remember anybody except Charley Davis."

Ross relaxed his hand and Willie slumped against the bar.

Everyone was thinking about what Willie had said and what it might mean. Their minds were dulled by the liquor, but not so dulled that they could not see how things were changed by Willie's information.

Liz Randall had a reason for being in the spot where they had found her. She went there to meet men, and even if there had been several of them, it wasn't likely that one of them had been Paco Morales. He was big, but he was still a kid.

Maybe they had been wrong.

"He probably knew she went out there," Ross said. "He laid for her and killed her. That's how it happened."

"What if the sheriff don't see it that way?" Case said.

"He'll see it that way. We'll make him see it that way," Ross said.

They all knew what they had to do, then. Ross was right. They had to make sure the sheriff didn't let anything change his mind about Paco; otherwise they were all going to look pretty damn bad for what they'd done.

"We better get down there and talk to him right now," Harper said. "He might've arrested Davis already."

"Right," Hawkins said. "We gotta be sure justice is done, see that the Morales kid is taken care of the right way."

They all had one last drink, and Harper took off his apron and came out from behind the bar.

"Anybody comes in here, Willie, you tell 'em the bar's closed," Harper said. "And you stay out from behind there."

"I won't bother anything," Willie said, and then he shut his mouth. He wanted to say more, but he just couldn't make himself. He wanted to tell them that they were making a big mistake, and he knew they were, but he couldn't say how he knew it. So he just kept his mouth closed and watched them walk out the door into the sunny street. They were walking pretty straight for men who had been drinking all morning, and they had their hats tilted slightly forward on their heads like men with a purpose.

The bottle Ross had been using was sitting right there on the bar where he had left it. Willie was pretty sure Ross had been drinking too much to remember how much was left in it. Anyway, he hoped so.

He pulled out the cork and poured himself a drink.

Chapter Fifteen

Paco Morales was gone when Sheriff Vincent got back to the jail with Jack and Charley.

Vincent knew the minute he walked in that something was wrong. The door to the cell block was wide open, and Vincent felt suddenly as if the world might be coming apart. It was bad enough that he'd just found out about Charley Davis courting Liz Randall, but now it looked like he'd lost his prisoner.

It was his own damn fault, naturally, going off like that and not even thinking twice about the fact that he had a prisoner in one of the cells and that it wouldn't be very smart to go running off down the street and leaving nobody in charge.

Even Jack could sense that something bad had happened. "That door ought not to be open, Sheriff," he said. "You told me never to leave it open if there was a prisoner in there."

"I didn't leave it open," Vincent said. "Somebody opened it." He turned to Charley.

"You sit down out here. I've got to check the cells. Jack, you keep an eye on him."

"Hey, I didn't do anything," Charley protested. "I'm the one that was gettin' shot at, remember?"

"Yeah. We'll talk about that in a minute. Now sit down." Vincent tried to make his voice sound tougher than he felt, because what he felt mostly was a hollow feeling right at the center of his belly, a hollowness that was spreading rapidly to fill his whole body. Everything was going wrong.

He walked through the door, not knowing what to expect, but what he found was even more surprising than anything he might have imagined. Instead of Paco Morales in the cell, there was Paco's mother.

She was sitting there calmly on the cot, her hands folded in her lap. She looked up at Vincent and smiled.

"Hello, Sheriff," she said. "You told me that I could come in this morning and see my son. But he is not here."

The key to the cell door was stuck in the lock of the wide open door.

"I knew I ought not to leave that key in my desk drawer," Vincent said, as much to himself as to the woman. "But then I didn't think Paco was going to be able to walk out of here. I'd heard you were somethin' of a healer, but you must be better than I thought."

"Perhaps the boy's fear gave him strength," Consuela said. "He was afraid that if he stayed here, he might die as unjustly as his father did."

Vincent wished that people would stop bringing up Paco's father. "You better find your boy, tell him to get on back here. It'll go easier with him at the trial if he does."

"The trial?" Consuela said. "Why are you so sure that there will be a trial?"

"It's the usual thing in murder cases," Vincent said.

"The man who shot my husband, he got a trial?"

Vincent shuffled his feet uncomfortably. "That was different," he said.

"Of course. I understand. That was just a case of a white man shooting a . . . a greaser. This time will be different, you tell me. But I am not so sure there will be a trial if you can find my son. There will be those who do not like the idea of giving him a fair chance, any more than his father was given one. When I saw him, he did not look as if he had been given much of a fair chance."

Vincent did not know what to say to the woman, mainly because she was coming unpleasantly close to the truth of the matter. Those fellas had beaten the boy unmercifully,

118

and they might've killed him if it hadn't been for Jack. He still found it hard to believe that Jack had stood up to them.

"You'd better go," he said finally, since he could think of nothing else.

"You do not want to arrest me?"

"No. I don't blame you for what you did. I'm just afraid it's going to make things rougher for the boy."

"If you can find him," Consuela said.

"Oh, I'll find him. You can count on that."

"We will see," she said, rising gracefully from the cot and walking past him and down the short hallway of the cell block. Before she went through the door and into the jail, she turned back.

"There is one more thing you should know," she said.

"What's that?"

"The girl who was killed had come to see me two weeks ago. She came more than once."

"What was the trouble?" Vincent said. "She sick?"

"No, she was not sick. But she wanted help, the kind of help I could not give to her."

"What kind of help was that?"

"She was going to have a baby. She did not want very much to have it."

Jesus, Vincent thought. It just gets worse and worse.

"Did she tell you who the father was?" he said.

"No. I did not ask her. That was no business of mine."

"Did her parents know?"

"They do now," Consuela said, and then she left.

"What was she doin' in there?" Jack asked when Vincent came back into the jail.

Vincent put the cell key in the desk and slammed the drawer shut. "Waitin' for us," he said. "To tell us she'd let her son out."

"Damn," Jack said.

"I wish somebody'd let me in on the secret of what's goin' on around here," Charley said. He was rolling a smoke, and when he was finished he scratched a lucifer on the sole of his boot. The match snapped into flame and he applied it to his cigarette, which flared briefly on the end before it settled to an easy glow. He fanned the match through the air until the flame was extinguished and then flipped the burned stick to the floor.

"Better pick that up," Jack said. "The sheriff likes a clean jail."

Charley looked doubtful, but he picked the matchstick up and put it in his pocket. He took a deep drag on his cigarette and let the smoke roll out of his mouth.

"Well," he said, "anybody gonna tell me?"

"It's about your sweetheart," Vincent said.

"Lucille?" Charley laughed. "She's got a temper, ain't she? But she'll cool down. You know how women are when they find out they ain't the only one in the world."

"That's the trouble," Vincent said. "Your *other* sweetheart."

Charley dropped his smoke to the floor and ground it under his boot. This time Jack did not admonish him.

"Oh," he said. "You mean Liz."

"That's who we mean, all right," Vincent said. "What about her?"

"What does that have to do with anything? I admit me and Lucille caused a stir in town, but there's no use draggin' that old business with Liz into it."

"Yeah, there is," Vincent said. He told him about Liz Randall.

"Goddamn," Charley said when the sheriff had finished. "Goddamn. You got any idea who did it?"

"Some people think it might've been Paco Morales," Jack said.

"Wasn't that his mother that just went out of here, the one you said let her son out?" Charley asked.

"The very same," Vincent told him.

"Well, why aren't you after him then? You

121

better get him before he gets away."

"Maybe he didn't do it," Vincent said. "He told me he was just on the way home from town and found the body."

"You gonna believe a Meskin kid? Hell, they lie just for the fun of it."

"Maybe," Vincent admitted. "But what if there was somebody else who wanted her dead, somebody who might've had a good reason to kill her?"

"Who you talkin' about?" Charley said. "Why are you lookin' at me like that?"

"'Cause I just found out that the Randall girl was pregnant," Vincent said.

Jack looked as shocked as Charley. "You sure about that?" he asked.

"No," Vincent said. "I'm not sure about anything right now. I've got to get hold of Doc Bigby and see what he has to say about it. Then maybe I'll know more about it." He looked at Charley. "You got anything you want to say on the subject?"

Charley was trying to roll another cigarette, but his hands were shaking too much. Tobacco flakes drifted down on his pants and to the floor.

"I . . . I don't reckon I do."

"Maybe you better think again, then," Vincent said. "You got any reason to believe that what I just said might be the truth, that the girl was pregnant?"

"It . . . it might be. I guess it could be. Hell, what do you want me to say?"

"I was thinkin' you'd say it was a crazy idea," Vincent told him. "But I guess that was too much to hope for."

"Listen," Charley said, giving up on the cigarette and putting the tobacco and papers away. "Does Lucille have to find out about this? She's already mad as a wet settin' hen, and if she finds out about this, no tellin' what she might do. She's already tried to kill me."

"I don't think she was really tryin'," Vincent said. "I expect she'll be tryin' a whole lot harder the next time she sees you." He thought for a minute. "Where were you last night, anyhow? Were you with Liz Randall?"

Charley looked down at the floor. "No," he said.

It was so obviously a lie that even Jack caught it, giving Vincent a look over Charley's shoulder.

Vincent was disgusted. "You saw her, all right. Did you kill her, Charley?"

"No!" Charley said. "I saw her, all right, but it was just to tell her to stop botherin' me. She was sendin' me notes out to the ranch but I'd already told her I was gonna marry Lucille. She never told me nothin' about any baby, though, I swear it."

"She tell you last night? Make you mad? Threaten you? Say she was goin' to tell Benteen? He'd've shot you dead on the spot if he knew."

"Mr. Benteen likes me," Charley said. "He wants me to marry his daughter."

"Looks like you've made a real mess of things, don't it?" Vincent said.

Charley opened his mouth to agree, but whatever he said was drowned out by the commotion outside the jail.

"See what's goin' on, Jack," Vincent said.

Jack walked over and opened the door. Outside were Harl Case, Turley Ross, Lane Harper, and Len Hawkins, all of them looking a little the worse for the morning's drinking. They were talking loud and cussing, jostling one another as they edged toward the doorway.

More trouble, Vincent thought. He got up and joined Jack.

"Mornin', fellas," he said. "What can I do for you?"

"You can give us that damn kid," Turley said. On the way over to the jail the men had decided to deal with matters directly, to demand Paco and mete out their own form of justice.

"Now, Turley, you know better than that," Vincent said. "I'll handle that kind of thing."

Turley pulled out his pistol. "We ain't foolin' around, Sheriff. Give us the damn kid."

"Put your gun up," Vincent said. "Come on in. You can have him if you can find him."

Chapter Sixteen

Hank Moran dusted off his pants and looked around the saloon. There was no one there except a lonely drunk holding up the bar, a half empty bottle by his elbow.

"Where is ever'body?" Moran asked. "People in Dry Springs quit drinkin'?"

"No liquor for sale here," Willie Turner informed him. "Bartender's out on business." The man looked familiar, but Willie couldn't place him.

"Looks like you're drinkin'," Moran said. He'd been riding for a while, and he was thirsty, even if it was a little earlier than he usually liked to start. For that matter, he usually didn't start at all. He liked to keep himself sharp and ready for anything at the card table.

He walked over to the bar. "How about sharin' a shot from that bottle?"

"It don't belong to me," Willie said, trying to focus on the man. "Don't I know you?"

"I might've been in here before," Moran

said, knowing damn well he had been. He had killed the Meskin here a few years back, right here in this self-same room. He glanced around. It looked pretty much the same as far as he could tell.

"You got any cardplayers in town?" he said.

"I know who you are now," Willie said, reaching for the bottle. It was like his nightmares coming true, the ones he had on the nights he wasn't dreaming about his wife and kid. It was like it was all happening again, and they had Paco Morales over in the jailhouse.

Moran leaned over the bar and looked around for a glass. He came up with one and took the bottle from Willie.

"If the bottle ain't yours, how come you're pourin' from it?" he said.

"It belongs to a friend," Willie told him.

"Any friend of yours is a friend of mine," Moran said, pouring a drink. He sipped it slowly, savoring the burn as it slid down his throat.

"Mighty good," he said when he finished. "Now, suppose you tell me where ever'body is this mornin'."

"Over to the jail, some of 'em," Willie said. "They told me to watch the place, not let anybody bother things. Told me to tell 'em the bar's closed."

"Well, you told me," Moran assured him. "What's goin' on over at the jail?"

Willie told him as much as he knew, and the information did not make Moran happy, especially the part about who Paco's father was. If the Meskin kid was accused of murder, it was bound to bring up all the old stories about how his father had died, stories that Moran would just as soon have remain buried in the past.

"Why's ever'body over there now?" Moran said.

"They want to hang the boy, I think," Willie said.

"Good idea, if you ask me. I don't think much of lettin' Meskins get away with killin' our women."

"You killed that boy's daddy and got away with it," Willie pointed out. Drinking sometimes made him say things he later wished he had left unsaid.

"He tried to kill me," Moran said. "He had a gun, tried to shoot me."

"It was a knife," Willie said. "He was supposed to have pulled a knife."

"Yeah, that's right. A knife. He was gonna cut me, like his kid cut up that woman."

"Looks like a man would remember the difference between a gun and a knife," Willie said.

Moran's hand drifted to the pistol he wore. "You tryin' to say somethin' funny?"

"No. Hell, no. Not me." Willie wished he would learn to keep his mouth shut. He hadn't said a word about that day to anyone in years, and now he was just blurting it all out to the one man he really didn't want to talk to about it.

Moran poured himself another drink. Willie didn't try to stop him. The gambler was wondering whether to drift on through or to stay and play cards. Maybe he ought to go on over to the jail and see what was happening. He set his glass down on the bar. That was what he would do.

He walked out of the saloon without another word to Willie, who was glad to see him go. Willie took the bottle by the neck and turned it up, not bothering with a glass. To hell with Turley. If he missed his liquor, Willie would be glad to pay him for it later. Right now he needed a drink about as much as he ever had.

And that was a lot.

Moran met the men on their way back from the jail. They were muttering among themselves and almost walked into him.

They all remembered the gambler, and he fell in with them as they walked back to the saloon.

"Mighty damn funny, you turnin' up here right now," Lane Harper said. "Almost spooky." Harper, like the others, had good reason to want to forget Moran. Seeing the gambler made him wonder about his own motives in the beating of Paco Morales, and he didn't like to question what he had done.

"Seems like ever' time you show up, we have us a little problem with the Meskins," Turley Ross said. He, too, did not like the feeling he got from seeing the gambler.

"Looks like this is one problem that's easy solved," Moran said. "Hang the boy and be done with it." If the boy was out of the way, he reasoned, things would settle down and he could relieve the citizens of some of their cash, just as he had originally intended to do.

"He oughta be hung," Len Hawkins said. "But it's hard to hang somebody you can't find."

"I thought he was in the jail," Moran said.

"Well, he ain't," Harl Case said. "He's escaped."

"Is the sheriff gettin' up a posse?" Moran asked.

The men stopped in their tracks. They hadn't thought about that. Too much morning drinking had addled their brains.

"Damn if he said a word about a posse," Hawkins said.

They stood in the street and thought about it. Around them the business of the town went on. Most people had not yet heard of the murder, or, if they had, they were trying to put it out of their minds.

"We could have us a posse of our own," Ross said. "We could go after him ourselves."

"Sure could," Hawkins agreed. "And we don't have to worry too much about bringin' him in alive."

Moran thought that was a good idea. "Hell, I'd go along with you. I like to see things done right."

"Way the sheriff was talking, he don't even think the kid done it," Harper reminded them.

"That's another reason we oughta do this," Case said. "See that things don't get outa hand. I've known Charley Davis awhile. I don't think he'd ever kill anybody, do you?"

None of them thought so, and they had to admit that the sheriff hadn't accused him. But it seemed as if the sheriff wanted Charley to stay around for a while. There was something between Charley and the girl that the sheriff didn't spell out.

"All right, we'll go after him, then," Ross said. "Let's get horses."

They started for the saloon again.

"Who's that comin' down the street?" Harper said. "Ain't that the preacher?"

"It is, for a fact," Ross said. "I wonder what he thinks of all this."

The Reverend Randall wasn't thinking much at all, not in the strict sense. He was walking along the street, the sun soaking into his black clothes, muttering to himself. He clutched his Bible in his left hand, and his right rested on the butt of an old pistol. None of the men could remember ever seeing the preacher with a gun before.

They stood waiting for him, but he didn't seem to see them there. He would have walked right into them if they had not parted and let him walk through their midst. His eyes looked straight ahead, staring at something only he could see.

"Hey, Preacher," Ross called as the man swept past them. "Wait a minute."

Randall appeared not to hear. He kept right on walking. Ross caught up with him and put a hand on his shoulder. The preacher shook him off impatiently, without turning.

Ross grabbed his arm, stopping him. Randall swung around, facing him.

"Preacher," Ross said, "where you goin'?"

"The jail," Randall said, his voice sounding hollow, as if he were talking to them from the bottom of a deep well. He jerked his arm from Ross's grasp and turned back toward the jail.

"That boy ain't there," Ross told him.

Randall stopped. "Not there? Where is he?"

"That's what we'd like to know," Ross said. "We're gettin' together a posse to go after him. You want to go with us?"

"'And if ye will not for all this hearken unto me, but walk contrary unto me, then I will walk contrary unto you also in fury; and I, even I, will chastise you seven times for your sins.'"

Lane Harper rubbed a hand across his thinning hair. "Does that mean yes?"

"'And he that killeth a beast, he shall restore it; and he that killeth a man, he shall be put to death.'"

"I figger that's a yes," Turley said. "You come on with us, Preacher. You got a horse?"

"'And he that killeth any man shall surely be put to death.'"

"That's exactly what we've been sayin' ourselves," Ross said. He put his big hand back on Randall's arm. "You go with us, and we'll find you a horse if you ain't got one."

He half dragged Randall along as they all headed back to the saloon together. Randall continued to talk, but he spoke in such a low voice that no one could quite make out the words.

He made Moran uncomfortable. What he was saying might come right out of the Bible, but it sounded more than a little crazy, the way the man was saying it.

If the others were bothered, however, they didn't show it, and Moran thought that they must know the preacher better than he did, being a stranger in town as he was. Besides, having your daughter killed by some damned Meskin was enough to make anybody a little crazy, and it never hurt to have the preacher on your side if you were doing something that the law might look on with a little disfavor. Though from what Moran remembered of the law in Dry Springs, they didn't have much to worry about. Just one broken-down old sheriff, with a deputy that was ugly as sin and not any better at being a lawman than the sheriff himself.

At first Moran had not experienced a good feeling about his return to Dry Springs. The murder of the girl threatened to spoil things for him. Now he was feeling better with each passing minute. If they could get the kid, they would have everyone in town on their side; they would be heroes. That would make a lot of them remember his killing of the boy's father, which now would be more of an asset than a liability. People would come to see him and to talk, and maybe he could get them into a friendly game.

Yes, indeed. It was beginning to look like the trip to Dry Springs was going to be a worthwhile one, after all.

Chapter Seventeen

Roger Benteen rode into town with ten men, stirring the dust on the dry street. It wasn't that he thought he needed them for anything. He could handle his daughter by himself. But he was used to having his men with him wherever he went. He didn't like to ride out alone, and he hadn't done it for years. It was as if having the riders along gave him a kind of authority that he might have lacked without them. The riders impressed people in a way that Benteen himself might not have been able to.

If they knew him, as everyone in Dry Springs assuredly did, they were impressed anyway, but he always took the riders. He may have felt he needed them because of his stature, which was decidedly unimpressive. He was no more than five feet tall, and that was with his high heeled boots on. Too, his face never frightened anyone or gave them cause to look on him with favor. Though he was nearly seventy years old, he still looked in some ways like a boy, with wide, curious eyes and a sensual, fill-tipped mouth. Those features, passed on to his daughter, merely added to her beauty and allure. On her father, they presented an oddly feminine aspect that belied his true nature.

For Roger Benteen was as ruthless as a starving timber wolf and as cold as a sidewinder. He could look at a man with those wide eyes and a smile on those full lips while at the same time plotting that man's downfall and ruin. He had not accumulated his fortune and his holdings by being as soft as he looked.

He had no plans to be soft with his daughter, either. She had never defied him before, and maybe she thought she could get away with it for that very reason. Maybe she thought that everyone deserved one defiant act.

Well, she was wrong. Roger Benteen was not going to tolerate even that much.

It was not that he was so fond of Charley Davis. True, Davis had shown he was a hard worker, and he appeared to be honest and at least moderately intelligent, but Benteen had once hoped for more for his only daughter. He did not like settling for second best, but when you lived on the edge of west Texas you had to take what you could get. It was a hard fact, and Benteen had grudgingly come to accept it.

So what he was left with was Charley. There were other cowhands, but Charley was the one who had showed the most drive and initiative when given the chance. Most of the breed moved around a lot, traveling from job to job, from ranch to ranch, never settling down on one for more than a few years at most.

Charley, however, had stuck it out with Benteen for four years now and showed no desire to move on. He had taken each new responsibility that Benteen offered him and made the most of it, and he had shown a quick grasp of every new task.

When Lucille began to notice the cowboy, Benteen could have stepped in. He chose not to because by then he knew that she wasn't going to do any better. Charley would never be the man that Benteen was, but maybe that didn't matter. He would be able to manage the ranch, with Lucille's guidance, of course, after Benteen was gone, and maybe that was good enough. He would never increase the holdings, but the odds were he would be able to hang on to what he had.

And now Lucille was threatening even that plan.

He couldn't figure what had come over the girl. One day she was making plans for her wedding, looking through magazines from back East at pictures of dresses, talking about what it would be like to have a house of her own. The next day she was running off and leaving her father a note saying that she was not going to marry Charley Davis, that she was moving into the Dry Springs Hotel, and that she was thinking about traveling to the East to see the world.

Benteen did not understand women; he understood men and cattle, or at least he liked to think that he did. His wife had died giving birth to Lucille, and he had never courted another. He had plenty of things to keep him busy, and he always discounted the stories of those men who said they could not go for more than a week without a woman. He figured they were either liars or stupid. He had gone for years, and it had never bothered him in the least, or never for more than a few minutes at a time.

Some of the boys had told him long before now that Charley had been seeing the preacher's daughter, that red-haired girl that Benteen had seen in town from time to time. He supposed she was pretty enough, though certainly not as pretty as Lucille. He could understand why Charley might like her.

That was all supposed to be over now, however. Charley had assured him that it was, and Benteen had never mentioned it to Lucille.

Maybe she had found out. If that was it, her behavior was probably normal for a woman, at least as far as Benteen knew. Anyway, it was something they could easily straighten out. Lucille would be home by that afternoon.

He and his men pulled up in a dust cloud in front of the hotel. He slid off his horse with an ease that belied his years and flipped a gold piece to one of the men.

"You fellas go on over to the saloon, have a drink on me," he said. "I'll give you a holler when it's time to go back to the ranch."

The men did not complain about being kept away from their work, and they certainly did not complain about the drinks. Benteen was not normally so free with his money, and in fact he had the reputation of something of a tight man with a dollar.

Benteen watched the men go, then stomped across the hotel boardwalk and entered the lobby.

The clerk, who had heard and seen him arrive, was practically standing at attention. "Good morning, Mr. Benteen. What can I do for you today, sir?"

Benteen turned his wide eyes on the young man. "You can tell me what room my daughter's in."

"Yes, sir. Two-oh-two, sir. Right at the head of the stairs."

Benteen didn't bother to thank the man. He walked past the desk and up the stairs.

He didn't bother to knock on the door of room 202, either, and he was angry when the knob failed to yield to his hand.

"Open this door, Lucille," he said. "You know who this is."

A key rattled in the lock and his daughter opened the door. Her eyes were red, and it appeared that she had been crying. Maybe she was coming to her senses already.

Benteen walked past her into the room. He always liked to keep a distance between them when they talked. Though he would never have admitted it, he was bothered by the fact that she was several inches taller than he was.

He walked to the window, then turned to face her. "Where's Charley?" he asked. "I know he came into town after you."

Lucille brushed at the corners of her eyes. "I . . . I don't know. The sheriff came and got him."

"The sheriff? What's he got to do with this?"

"There was a little shooting," Lucille admitted. "I guess it stirred things up a little."

Benteen raised an eyebrow, a trick that had always irritated Lucille. "A little shooting? Who was doing it?"

"I guess I was."

"And who did you shoot?"

141

"Nobody. I was shooting at Charley, but I didn't mean to hit him."

It didn't make sense to Benteen. "If you were doing the shooting, why was Charley the one who was arrested?"

"I don't know," Lucille said. "I think it has something to do with that Randall girl, but I couldn't hear what they were saying."

Benteen couldn't figure it out, but that didn't matter. It could wait until he could speak to the sheriff. Right now he had to talk some sense into his daughter.

"I don't know what gets into you, girl," he said. "You're throwin' away the chance to marry the best man in Dry Springs by behavin' like this."

"Ha!" Lucille said. "A man that sneaks around and meets another woman behind my back? I'd think I was well rid of someone like that."

"Who told you he was doing that?" Benteen asked. He knew that he had not spoken of it. He had done his best to keep it quiet.

Lucille, who had heard the news from one of the ranch hands, was not about to tell where she had gotten the word. She knew her father too well for that. "Never mind," she said. "I heard, and that's enough."

"It doesn't matter," Benteen said, thinking that he could get it out of her later. He wasn't going to keep a hand who didn't know when to shut his mouth. "The point is that Charley's long past havin' anything to do with that girl. He's not interested in anybody but you now."

"Yes, he is. He saw her again just last night."

"What?" Benteen hadn't known that.

"It's true. You ask him." Lucille had the information from a good source. She had been looking for Charley early in the evening, and she was told where he had gone by the same cowboy who had told her about Charley and Liz in the first place. The cowboy had for some time had a crush on Lucille, and he couldn't resist the chance to get Charley in trouble.

"I'll see about that later, too," Benteen said. "Right now, you're goin' to get your things and get back out to the ranch." He looked at the valise beside the bed.

"I'll go when I'm ready," Lucille said. "You think I ought to take Charley just because he's the only man around here you like. Well, there might be better men somewhere else. I might just go look."

Benteen could see that getting Lucille home was not going to be as easy as he had hoped. She had always had a stubborn streak in her, she got it from her mother. But that was all right. Sooner or later she would give in.

"I'm goin' to see the sheriff, see what he

has to say about this shootin' business," he said. "You stay here until I come back for you."

Lucille nodded. She did not have anywhere to go at the moment, and she had already checked on the stage schedule. There would not be a coach coming through Dry Springs until the next day.

She had thought about living in the hotel, but she could see now that there would be no escaping her father as long as she was in town. She tried to remember where the stage was going.

Benteen went out of the room, leaving the door open behind him. Lucille closed it. She was beginning to wish she had gone ahead and shot Charley. Then it would all be over with, one way or another.

She had to admit, at least to herself, that the more she thought about it, the less attractive marriage to him seemed. He was handsome enough, no doubt about that, and he did have those pretty blue eyes, but there was really nothing to him. He was a good worker, an honest enough man, but that was all. Somehow she had expected something more, and obviously she wasn't going to find it in Dry Springs.

Charley's attitude toward women was typical, she thought. He could have her for his wife, but he still could not resist looking around at whatever else was available, and he didn't seem to see anything wrong with that.

Well, it *was* wrong, and she was not going to put up with it. He could try pretty words on her, but it wouldn't work, not any more.

Suddenly the stage's destination popped into her head. San Antonio. She knew no one there, knew nothing about the place, but there were probably trains from there to all over the country. She wondered how long her money would last.

Long enough, she decided, so that she would never have to see Charley Davis again.

Chapter Eighteen

Martha Randall burst into the sheriff's office, looking wildly around her. "My husband," she said. "Where's my husband?"

"He ain't around here," Vincent said. "Is he supposed to be?"

"I don't know," she said. "I thought he might be." She looked around and saw Jack and Charley. "I'm sorry I bothered you all. I'll go look for him."

She eased back out the door, quite a trick for someone of her size.

"Wait a minute," Vincent said. "Somethin's the matter. You want to tell me about it?"

She looked at Charley and Jack again.

"Maybe you two oughta go take a look at the cells," Vincent suggested.

"Oh," Jack said. "Yeah. Come on, Charley." They went through the door into the cell block and closed it behind them.

"I didn't mean to chase anybody off," Mrs. Randall said.

"It's all right," Vincent told her. He would

have asked her to sit down, but he was afraid she wouldn't fit into the only chair. "Charley needs to get a look at a cell, anyway." He didn't offer to explain why. "Now, what about your husband?"

"He's acting funny," she said. "That Mrs. Morales, she told him that Liz was . . . was . . ."

"Goin' to have a baby," Vincent said. "She told me that same thing. I haven't checked with the doc yet."

"I think my husband believed it," she said. "He called Liz the Whore of Babylon."

"He called his daughter that?"

"He was quoting from the Bible," she said. "But . . ."

Vincent waited. He didn't know how to help her.

After a minute she went on. "He didn't seem surprised like he should've been. Like I was. And he kept talkin' about punishment, about an eye for an eye."

"What do you think he meant?"

Mrs. Randall shook her head. "I don't know. But I was wonderin' — it's terrible to think this — but I was wonderin' if he . . . if he could've been the one that killed Liz."

It took Vincent a second or two to let what she said sink in, and even then he wasn't quite sure he'd heard right. He had to say it out loud to be sure.

"You think your husband killed your daughter?"

"I just don't know. He's talkin' funny, and he's got a funny look in his eyes. So I was wonderin' —"

"Wasn't he at home with you last night?"

"He was for most of the time, but right before supper he always goes out to take the air, if the weather's good. He says he likes to pray in the outdoors, says it lets him feel closer to God if he's out there in creation. Last night was one of those nights he went out."

"Did he know about your daughter?"

"I don't know, Sheriff. I used to think I knew him, but now I wouldn't even try to say. If you'd asked me that yesterday, I'd've said no, he didn't know a thing. It seemed to me he was a lot more in the dark about this than even I was. Now, though, I just don't know. When I think about it, I wonder if maybe he did know somethin' and just kept quiet about it. He was the kind of man that could keep quiet if he wanted to. A preacher's got to be like that."

Vincent was sure that his stomach was going to tie itself in a square knot. It wasn't bad enough that he had people wanting to hang Paco Morales for killing Liz Randall; now he had Charley Davis, who had maybe got the dead girl pregnant, and the girl's own daddy who might've found out about her habits and killed her himself.

"Why did you think he might be here?" he said.

"He went out of the house wearin' a gun," she said. "Sheriff, I don't think he's had that gun on in all the years we've been married, but he strapped it on today."

"That wouldn't mean he was comin' to the jail, though," Vincent pointed out.

"It was that eye-for-an-eye business," she said. "I got the idea that if his girl was dead, then he was goin' to see that somebody else died, too."

"If he killed her himself, why would he want to kill the Morales boy?"

She shook her head. "I can't say, Sheriff. Who knows what might be goin' on in the head of a . . . a crazy man."

Vincent looked at her sharply, but she didn't look away.

"I know I oughtn't to say it, not about my own husband, but it's the truth," she said. "He's gotten worse and worse over the years, the way he's treated Liz, the way he's treated me. I guess I should've seen it comin', but I never did." She paused. "It's too late for Liz. It's even too late for me. But it might not be too late for the boy. You got him locked up safe and sound?"

"No," Vincent said. "I don't."

"Then you better find my husband, Sheriff, before he uses that gun he put on."

Vincent sighed. "I'll try," he said.

The Reverend Randall could feel the gun riding on his hip. It felt strange there, in a way, but in another way it felt as familiar as the burn of the sun through his black suit.

He had worn the gun constantly at one time, and even now he took it down once a week from the peg where it hung and gave it a good cleaning with an oiled rag. He still believed in taking care of the things that could take care of him.

There had been a time when he had used the pistol often and accurately, gaining a reputation and a name — Kid Reynolds. It was a name he had long abandoned. Kid Reynolds was dead, or that was what everyone believed, those who thought of him at all, and those were probably few indeed.

Even to Randall, at least until today, Kid Reynolds was dead, a person who was no more to him than a dim memory, more like someone he had once met than someone he had once been.

After all, it had been more than twenty-five

years ago when he had been shot up by two men who laid for him one night when he was leaving the cribs behind some saloon in some town whose name he no longer recalled. They were looking for him in the matter of their brother's death, the result of a gunfight that Reynolds had won only a few days before.

The young man — they were both no more than eighteen — had called him out, and Reynolds had gone, eager to build on his growing reputation with a pistol. He shot the man in front of witnesses, all of whom were willing to swear that the fight had been provoked, and thought no more about it after he had accepted the congratulations and the drinks that went along with the victory. It wasn't the first time he'd been involved in that kind of shoot-out.

The brothers had not bothered to call him out, however, had not given him a chance, not even so much as a warning. They shot him in the back and left him for dead, which is very nearly what he had been, and what he certainly would have been had not a half-crazy old man who called himself Elijah and who thought of himself as a reincarnation of that Old Testament prophet happened upon him, taken him home, and nursed him back to health with a combination of frenzied prayer and a shrewd knowledge of how to care for gunshot wounds.

It had been touch and go for a while, and Reynolds had been delirious for much of two days with pain and fever, two days during which Elijah sat beside the bed and alternately read aloud from the scriptures and drank from a bottle of rotgut that he kept handy. It was some of the same whiskey that he used to sterilize Reynolds's wounds.

Somehow the kid gunfighter had been touched by the old man's madness, had in his fever dreams become, like the old man, a fervent believer in the Word. When his fever broke, he was filled with the desire to preach, to reach out to sinners and touch them the way that he had been touched, and he never put on his gun again, taking the name Randall and swearing to carry a Bible in his hand instead of a weapon.

Now a new kind of delirium had settled on him, a delirium that had been brought about in part by what he regarded as his daughter's betrayal of him, though it was a delirium that had been growing over the years without his even being aware of it. His wife was right; it had expressed itself in his treatment of her and their daughter, the old wildness finding an outlet in words and more subtle actions than the firing of a gun.

He saw things now as through a glass darkly, and he had become something different from either the wild young gunfighter that he had been so long ago or the preacher that he had been for the past twenty-five years.

He was neither one nor the other now, but rather some strange creature that even he did not understand and could not have explained if asked.

He knew only that his daughter was dead and that vengeance was demanded. He had preached a gospel of love, and that had failed him. That had brought him nothing more than a wife grown grossly fat and a daughter who was a scarlet whore.

It never occurred to him to wonder if it was possible that he had failed the gospel rather than the other way around. He had been sure for so long that he was in the right that the idea he might be wrong had never disturbed his consciousness until very recently.

The daughter had paid for her sins. Now it was someone else's turn. These men he was with, Ross and the others, they seemed to know what they were about, and it seemed to fit in with his own desires, as much as he understood them. Everything was confused and spinning in his head, and he no longer had a clear destination in mind. It had seemed simple at first: go to the jail, kill the boy who was being held there, and then face down any man who called him out. That was what he would have done in the old days.

But now they were telling him that the boy was no longer there, that he had escaped. No one seemed to know where he was, but they were going to find him.

Randall would go with the men then, and he would serve as an instrument of God's judgment. It was all that there was left for him to do.

A thought flashed into his mind. Perhaps that was what he had been before, in the days when he wore the gun. An instrument of God's vengeance, smiting the unrighteous.

He remembered what the men had said to Joshua: "'Whosoever he be that doth rebel against thy commandment, and will not hearken unto thy words in all that thou commandest him, he shall be put to death: only be strong and of a good courage.'"

Perhaps that was right, and he was like Joshua, sent to be a right arm of God and meant to be obeyed by all, to punish by putting to death all those who did not listen to his words and obey his commandments.

People like his daughter, people like Paco Morales.

If that was true, then he had actually failed his calling when he put down his gun and took up the Bible. He had wasted twenty-five years.

But he had returned to the calling now.

God would be merciful.

God would forgive him if he was strong and of good courage.

He let his hand stroke the smooth wooden handle of the pistol, and it felt good. It felt right.

Randall smiled.

Chapter Nineteen

Paco had made it to his house, but he wasn't sure just how he had gotten there. More than once he had been pretty sure he would never make it, but he kept going. His mother had told him the men would kill him if he stayed in the jail, and he had believed her.

They had killed his father, and they would kill him.

He did not enter his home when he got there, however. He went first to the well and drew up a bucket of water, pulling the rope with one arm and thinking again of the times when he had gone there to wait and get water for the mule when one of his mother's visitors was in the house.

He got the bucket up to the top of the well and looped the rope around a nail to hold it there. He managed to lean out and get his hand on the bucket and pull it to him. Then he bent his knees and tilted the bucket so the water spilled out, running into his mouth and down his chin, chilling him as it soaked into his shirt.

When he had drunk his fill, he hobbled over to the shade of a mesquite tree and awkwardly sat down. His ribs hurt, and his arm, but it was nothing he could not bear.

He thought that his sisters might be watching him from the house, but he did not call out to them. He leaned back against the tree and closed his eyes to wait on his mother, or whoever came to find him.

He might have slept, for it seemed like no time at all had passed before he looked up to see his mother standing over him, looking down into his face.

"You cannot stay here," she said. "Not out in the open like this."

"It would not be safe for me to stay in the house," he pointed out. "Maybe I should catch the mule and ride toward Mexico." He had no idea how far away Mexico might be, but he knew he could never ride there, not even if it was only five miles. However, he did not want to bring trouble to his home.

His mother smiled. "You are a foolish boy, but I forgive you. You must stay here."

"But where?"

They had no barn, but there was a small shed that his father had built to keep his tools in. Paco had played in the shed when he was younger, and even then it had seemed cramped.

He struggled to his feet. "They will find me there as easily as if I were in the house."

"Perhaps not. Come."

They walked to the shed, made of warped boards and lacking even a window for light. There was no fastener on the door.

Consuela opened the door and the sunlight fell inside. Dust motes swirled in the light. There was a stack of wooden boxes, most of them empty, a rake, a hoe with a broken handle, a plowshare and plow lines, and a heap of something that looked like a dead animal. It was an old buffalo robe that Paco's father had come by somehow years before.

There was nothing else in the shed, but it was so small that even those few things that were there crowded it. It was hot, and Paco could feel his breath being sucked away before he even got inside.

"Go ahead," Consuela said. "Get in."

Paco obeyed her reluctantly. The only place to sit was in the middle of the floor, on the robe. He sat, trying to breathe the burning air. When he did, the dust tickled the inside of his nose and he sneezed. He brushed his sleeve across his nose.

"I will bring your father's rifle," Consuela said. "I hope that you will not have to use it."

"They will come for me," Paco said. "I hurt no one, but they will come. If they come, I will use the rifle."

"We will try to trick them," Consuela said. "I will take the mule away and tie it, but not well. Just enough so that it will stay for a while before it gets free. Perhaps they will see that the mule is gone and believe you are on it. If we are lucky, they will follow it."

"It will come home," Paco said.

"Not at once. Time will pass. Perhaps the sheriff will find the man who did the thing they accuse you of."

Paco did not have much faith in that possibility. "What if they do come to the shed?" he asked. "Then shall I use the rifle?"

"Then you should cover yourself with the robe. Put the boxes in front of the door and make yourself small. Pull the robe over you. They will not see you."

Paco did not think that would work, but he would do as his mother said. If they pulled the robe away, however, he would shoot. He would not let them kill him and walk away smiling the way they had done when they killed his father. This time, they would pay.

His mother closed the door and went to the house. Paco sat with his eyes wide open, trying to accustom them to the darkness which at first seemed absolute.

Eventually, however, he could see the light that shone through the cracks between the boards, and then he could see the vague outlines of the boxes and the tools.

When his mother opened the door, the sudden glare almost blinded him, and he vowed to himself to keep his eyes on the cracks from then on, to let them take in as much light as they could. He did not want to miss his first shot.

"Here," Consuela said, handing him the rifle. It was a lever-action Henry that was older than Paco.

She put four cartridges into his hand. "That is all the ammunition we have," she said.

"It will be enough," he told her.

She said nothing, closing the door. Then she went to catch the mule.

Vincent had no call to hold Charley at the jail, so he let him go, telling him to stay in town. He left Jack in charge of the jail — too late, he knew, but he wasn't going off and leave the place unattended this time. He had to talk to Bigby and to try to find Paco.

Bigby was his usual ebullient self again, smiling and showing his teeth all the way back to his throat when Vincent entered the office, really nothing more than a rented room decked out with a few ads for patent medicines on the wall.

"I took the girl over to Rankin's, like you said. He wasn't too happy with me for bringin' her in, though. Said she was a real mess, and he didn't have time to fix her like she ought to be fixed, not with the weather as hot as it is. I told him the family'd be by to talk to him about the buryin'."

He stopped to look to Vincent for approval, and when the sheriff did not say anything, Bigby went on.

"Did I do the right thing? You did say the family'd best see her over there, didn't you? Told me not to keep her here?"

"That's right," Vincent said. "But I'm not sure the family ever went over there, at least not the father. Maybe the mother did. Anyway, that's not why I'm here."

"Well, well. Don't tell me you've got somethin' the matter with you. It'd be the first time. You comin' down with a cold or the fever? I got some medicines here that'll have you feelin' better in no time." He started rummaging around in his bag, the bottles clinking together.

"I don't need anything like that," Vincent said.

"Well, what do you need, then? I hate to say it, Sheriff, but it ain't like you to be droppin' by for a sociable visit. There must be somethin' on your mind."

"There is," Vincent said.

"You're sure havin' a hard time sayin' what it is, ain't you? One of those 'delicate' matters, is it?"

"That's right," Vincent said. "It's delicate. That's the right word."

Bigby rubbed his hands together. "You come to the right man, then. Bein' a doctor and all, I can keep quiet about things when I have to. People wouldn't tell me what I need to know to help 'em otherwise."

Where had he heard something just like that lately? Vincent wondered, and then remembered that Martha Randall had said practically the same thing about her husband. As far as Vincent knew, it was the only thing doctors and preachers had in common.

"It's about the girl," Vincent said.

"What about her? She's dead, that's all."

"Was she pregnant?"

Bigby's smile went from wide to thin, but he didn't say anything.

"I thought that was one of the things you'd check, just to be sure, in a case like this. It's just what a doctor ought to do."

"You sayin' I ain't a doctor?"

"I'm just asking, did you check. That's all."

"What if I did?"

"Then you can answer me. Was she pregnant?"

"Yeah," Bigby said. "Yeah, she was."

"Dammit, then why didn't you tell me to start with? You can't keep somethin' like that a secret."

"Why not?" Bigby said. "Why the hell not? She was the preacher's girl! How do you think her mama and daddy will feel if they find out she was gonna have a baby?"

"It might've been better for them to hear it from you or me than the way they heard it," Vincent said, not saying what that way was. "You should've told me, Doc."

Bigby looked shamefaced. "I know it. Hell, I started to, but I thought, maybe I could save the family from knowin'. It seemed like the right thing."

"All right. We won't argue about it. But that changes things a little as far as Paco Morales is concerned."

"How's that?"

"Gives us another suspect," Vincent said. "Rankin know about this?"

"I didn't tell him. He won't figure it out for himself. He'll just be wantin' to get her in the ground."

"He may have to wait awhile," Vincent said.

Chapter Twenty

On their return from the jail, the men slammed into the saloon where Willie Turner was drinking with Benteen's cowhands, who had not been put off in the least by the fact that Willie told them there was no one there to sell them any liquor. They were not going to be denied their chance for a drink, and they went behind the bar for what they wanted, ignoring Willie's pleas to leave. When he saw that there was no use in arguing with them, he joined them.

He had just about finished off Ross Turley's bottle, though it hadn't done him any good. For some reason, he couldn't seem to get drunk, not even halfway. The more he drank, the more sober he got. It wasn't a good feeling.

A couple of the girls who lived out back had come in by now, and things were getting pretty lively by the time the men came back from the jail, what with the liquor being supplied by Benteen. Willie wasn't joining in the fun, but the cowhands weren't letting that bother them. They were laughing and joking, playing up to the girls and pinching them on the sly, not that it seemed to bother the girls all that much. They were laughing, too, probably hoping to engage in a cash transaction or two later on, when things got to rolling really good.

"What's goin' on here?" Lane Harper demanded as he came through the doors. He looked for Willie and saw him standing at the bar between two of the waddies. "I thought I told you —"

"I know what you told me," Willie said. "I tried to get 'em to leave. You can ask 'em." He wondered what the preacher was doing there, all dressed in black like he was ready for church. It didn't seem right for a preacher to be in a saloon, not where there were girls and drinking. The gambler was with them, too. Willie didn't like the gambler being there. That wasn't a good sign.

"Leave him be," Len Hawkins advised. "We got other things to discuss."

Harper wasn't going to be dissuaded so easily. "If Mr. Danton was to've come in here and seen all this goin' on and me bein' gone, he'd sack me quick as a cat can lick its ass. I oughta —"

"Mr. Danton ain't comin' in," Turley Ross said. "When's the last time he came in here, anyway?"

Harper didn't say anything to that. He knew exactly the last time Danton had come in. It had been the day the gambler, that same fella who was with them now, had killed Morales. Danton had been there then, and what happened had sort of killed the pleasure he took in coming in. He had been back, of course. It was his business. But he came in only when he had to, and he didn't stay long when he was there. He didn't even mess with any of the girls anymore.

"Let 'em have a little fun," Ross said. "Let's decide what we're gonna do about that kid."

"Let's us have a little fun, too," Harl Case said. "Get us a drink, Lane."

Harper went behind the bar and got a bottle. Willie was glad to see that Ross seemed to have forgotten that he had already bought one.

The men went to a table and pulled up some chairs. They sat down, opened the bottle, and began discussing their next move. Willie noticed that although the preacher sat down, he didn't have anything to say, nor did he touch the bottle. And Willie saw the gun the preacher was wearing. He'd never seen anything like that before, and he knew it meant trouble, even more trouble than there was already.

Then Charley Davis came in, and the trouble got worse. It seemed to Willie as if he could almost predict what was going to happen, like he could see the future.

Davis would tell the ranch hands what had happened to Liz Randall, and they would be indignant. The men over at the table, their heads together, would hear the cowboys talking, and because they felt the same way, everyone would get together. Willie couldn't see beyond that, but he knew that nothing good would come of it.

He was right. It happened pretty much that way, with two exceptions. One of them Willie didn't know about, since he didn't realize that Charley was a suspect in the case. Charley left that part out entirely, making it sound as if Paco Morales was guilty beyond a doubt.

The other exception was the way the upstairs girls reacted. Willie hadn't thought about them. They pretended to be afraid and put their hands to their mouths and talked about how a girl "couldn't even go out for so much as a little walk without getting killed by some crazy Meskin."

It was almost sickening to listen to them, but Willie did listen. He seemed frozen at the bar, his head icily clear despite the liquor he had drunk. He looked at Turley's bottle. It was empty, but that didn't seem to matter now. Willie didn't want any more. It was useless to him now.

"We oughta do somethin' about it," one

of the ranch hands, a big, broad-shouldered man named Frank, said.

"Damn right. We oughta go down to the jail and tell the sheriff what we think about a town where a decent woman can't even walk outside without fearin' for her life," another cowhand said.

"You'll have to do better than that," Ross said from the table. He was glad to hear the commotion, and he was already thinking about how it could benefit his own ideas. "The one that did it's already out of the jail."

"You mean the sheriff let him out?" Frank said.

"No," Charley told him. "The kid escaped."

"That damn sheriff never was no good," Frank muttered. "I guess there's nothin' we can do, then."

"Sure there is," Ross said. He was about to tell them what they could do when the bat-wings swung inward and Roger Benteen entered the saloon.

The noise level dropped to nothing. Everyone looked at Benteen, even the men from town. They knew that he pretty much ran things around here, and they didn't know how much he knew about the situation.

He didn't know anything, of course, but Davis drew him aside and filled him in quickly, once again leaving out any hint that he might be involved with Liz Randall's death.

Benteen was not a stupid man, however. "Goddamn, Charley. Did you have anything to do with this?"

"Hell, no," Charley said. "You know I wouldn't be mixed up in something like that. Ever'body says the Morales kid did it." He was beginning to see that if he could shift the blame entirely to the Morales boy, he would be in the clear.

"Any evidence to that effect?" Benteen liked to think of himself as a law-abiding man.

"Those fellas saw him do it," Charley said, pointing over to Turley Ross and the others.

"The preacher saw his own daughter killed?" Benteen found that hard to believe.

"No, sir, he wasn't with 'em, but those others, they saw it. You ask 'em."

"I will," Benteen said, and he did.

Ross eagerly confirmed everything, and Benteen went back to Davis. "We've got to do something about this. Lucille's just on the verge of doing something crazy, and this might just push her over the edge, since you were involved with the girl. Ross tells me that the boy's escaped from the jail, besides."

"That's right," Davis said. "The way I saw it, his mama came and let him out while the sheriff was busy calmin' Lucille down."

"That's where he'll be, then," Benteen said.

"At home with his mama. From what Ross says, he was in pretty bad shape."

"I guess so," Davis said. He had an idea what was coming.

So did Willie. You could feel it in the room, like it was something in the air. Benteen's men had all had just about enough to drink to make them a little wild, and some of the others had been drinking, too, earlier. It didn't matter that what they were about to decide to do was wrong. That wouldn't even enter into it, since they would convince themselves that they were right.

And Willie knew he wasn't going to try to stop them, though he should. There were powerful reasons why he should, but he just couldn't get them clear in his mind.

There were some in the room who had not been drinking and whose minds were not clouded that way, but they were mixed up in other ways, by their own reasoning, in fact.

Hank Moran. He wanted to get the kid out of the way so he could get down to the business of relieving the town's citizens of their spare money. And if the kid was guilty, it would practically prove that Moran had been innocent in killing the father years before, or so it seemed to the gambler.

Charley Davis didn't want word to get out about Liz's condition. If it did, his marriage to Lucille Benteen was over before it ever took place. Lucille, of course, would be devastated, and her father would probably kill him. But if the kid was dead, he would become the guilty party out of necessity. Even the sheriff would have to go along, and maybe no one would ever find out that Liz had been pregnant when she died.

Benteen's case was different. He just wanted to catch the guilty party and show his daughter that Charley Davis had long ago broken any connection with a girl who met with others in the evening.

And if you had asked Randall why he was there or what he was going to do, he probably couldn't have told you. His hand kept going to the butt of the pistol at his hip, caressing the smooth wood as if it were a woman's skin. He sat at the table and listened to the men talking, but he did not take part. His eyes were on them, but he wasn't seeing them. He seemed almost to be looking right through them, as if seeing something that no one else in the room was privileged to see.

He did speak occasionally, but not in response to anything anyone else said. He wasn't talking to them. They didn't know who he was talking to, and they were afraid to ask.

He said things like, "'For the great day of his wrath is come, and who shall be able to stand?'" It was clearly a question, but no one tried to answer it. For the most part, they simply looked away from him, as if he had done something slightly embarrassing.

The talk in the big room grew in volume, rising like the growing rumble of thunder that signals a summer storm. Booted feet shuffled on the plank floor. Spurs jingled. Bottles clinked against glasses.

Finally Turley Ross's voice cut through the noise. "Let's go get him. That's what we've gotta do."

It might not have been what they *had* to do, but it was what they wanted to do, what they had been urging themselves to do all morning, whether they realized it or not.

Willie had known it long before they had said it aloud, but he still groaned when he heard it.

"That's a good idea," Benteen said. "We'll bring him in."

Benteen's voice settled it for all of them. If Benteen was in it, they were all in it, and they all understood him to imply more than his words actually said.

What they understood was that they were going after Paco Morales. Whether they actually brought him in or not was another thing.

They might really do it. But if he tried to resist, well, they would just have to see what might happen in a case like that. If he tried to resist, the kid just might find himself getting killed.

No one said it aloud, but it was in the air of the room like the stink of death, and Willie Turner could hardly breathe.

Chapter Twenty-One

After he left Bigby's office, Vincent decided he'd better go looking for Paco. He was worried about that bunch that had left the jail, but he thought they were likkered up and probably wouldn't do anything foolish. They might try to work themselves up to it, but in the end they were decent men who would do the right thing.

He didn't take into account the possibility that they might meet up with another group of like-minded men. Had he done so, he would have gone by the saloon to check on them. He knew that while one or two men might think about doing something foolish, they would rarely act on the thought, whereas a bunch of men got braver in proportion to their numbers.

He also didn't realize that Roger Benteen was in town and would be one of the group. Benteen was the kind of man who could easily sway men to one side or the other on an issue.

So, not having any idea of what was going

on in the saloon, Vincent went down to the stable and saddled up for his ride out to the Morales place without worrying too much about what might happen. What was worrying him was whether Paco was guilty or not.

There was that business about Charley, for one thing. If there was anybody that had a reason to kill Liz Randall, it was him. Marrying Benteen's daughter was the best thing that Charley could ever have hoped for from life, and considering how Lucille was taking the news that Charley had just been seeing the girl, she wouldn't like it worth a damn if she found out the girl was pregnant.

Vincent tightened the girth. By God, he thought. What if she *did* know? If she was shooting at Charley, intending to miss, what might she have done to the woman?

He swung up into the saddle, wondering if he should go by the hotel and ask her, but he thought better of it. If she did know, he'd find out sooner or later. If she didn't, he damn sure wasn't going to be the one who told her.

He'd better ride by the jail, though, and let Jack know where he was going. That Jack was a case now, standing up to those men the way he had. As far as Vincent knew, that was the first time Jack had ever done anything like that. He was shy about his face, about his eye and all, and it made him hesitate to use his authority.

And that gave Vincent another thought. Jesus God, could it be possible? Hell, in this mess, anything could be possible. He'd better get to the jail and talk to Jack about it, though he didn't see how he could bring the subject up.

It turned out to be easier than he thought. It took him awhile to work up to the subject, but he got it done.

"Jack," he said, "I been thinkin' about when that girl was killed."

The two men were in the jail again, Vincent seated at the desk. He had tied his horse outside and gone in, making the excuse that he wanted to check something with Jack about the murder, which was true enough anyway.

"Sure," Jack said. "What about it, Sheriff?"

"Well, I know you told me somethin' about the girl last night, somethin' about how you saw her over at that grove not long before the killin'. Now, Jack, those trees, they just don't happen to be in your usual territory."

Jack frowned, clearly puzzled by the turn of the conversation. He didn't seem to get the point.

"What I mean is, you check around town and sometimes you check out a few of the houses, but you don't get out that way much. It's not very close to the area you're supposed to be patrollin'. So I was wonderin' . . ."

Jack got it then. He got up out of the chair where he'd been sitting and walked over to the cell-block door without saying anything.

"You see where I'm goin' with this, Jack?" Vincent asked.

"Yeah, I see," Jack said reluctantly.

"And you see why I've gotta ask you?"

Jack nodded. He could see that, too, but it didn't make things any easier for him.

He wasn't making things any easier for Vincent by keeping his mouth shut, either. The sheriff gave him a few seconds to respond, but Jack still had nothing to say.

"Well, Jack," Vincent said. "Looks like I'm gonna have to ask you straight out — did you ever meet that Randall girl yourself?"

At first he thought his deputy was not going to answer, but finally Jack said, "Yeah. Yeah I met her a time or two."

Vincent was surprised. He had thought it might be possible, but he really didn't believe it. After all, Jack, with his face and all, didn't seem like the kind of man a romantically inclined young woman would be interested in, no matter how much her father tried to keep her penned up in the house.

Besides, Vincent prided himself on the way

he kept up with things in town, and he was finding out there was a lot going on that he didn't know a thing about. He knew Liz Randall was roaming around, but he sure didn't know who she was meeting. His own deputy, too. It was hard to believe.

Jack didn't seem to have anything else to offer, so Vincent said, "I'm waitin', Jack."

Jack walked back to the chair and sat down. "It wasn't nothin' like you're thinkin'. I just met her to talk to a couple of times, that's all."

"You weren't the only one, by a long shot."

"That's the truth," Jack said. "There was me, and I guess there was Charley. She never mentioned him, though."

"Anybody else?"

"Willie Turner. She'd talk to him now and then."

Willie Turner? Vincent thought. This was getting stranger by the minute. Was there anybody in town the girl hadn't seen while she was out walkin' after dark?

"What about Willie?" he said.

"Nothin' much. She just asked me about him. Asked me if it was true about the way his wife and kid died. I think he cried on her shoulder now and then."

"You shoulda told me this sooner, Jack."

"I know it, Sheriff. I just thought . . . I don't know what I thought. When I saw she was dead, I felt so bad, and then there was the Morales boy. Ever'body was yellin' that he done it, and it was all confusin'."

"You stopped 'em from killin' him," Vincent said. "Why'd you do that, Jack?"

Jack looked puzzled again. "What d'you mean?"

"What I said. Why'd you stop 'em?"

"'Cause it was wrong. He mighta done it, but there was no call for them to string him up. He oughta have a trial, just like anybody. You know that."

"And that's the only reason?"

"What other reason would there be?" Jack said.

Vincent didn't answer him. He was wondering if Jack had stopped them because he knew Paco was innocent, knew it because maybe he'd been the one to kill the girl. Suppose he'd made advances to her and she'd laughed at him, said somethin' about his face. There were men who'd killed for less than that, though Jack didn't seem like the kind to do it.

"No other reason," Vincent said, getting up from behind the desk. "You did the right thing, Jack. I'm proud of you."

"Thanks, Sheriff," Jack said. He got up, too, and walked to the door of the jail with Vincent.

"I'm goin' to see about Paco," Vincent said.

"You stay here, but don't tell anybody where I'm gone. Just say I'll be back soon."

"Right," Jack said. "I got it, Sheriff."

Vincent slipped the reins off the hitch rail and swung himself up into the saddle. The leather creaked as he settled himself, and he rode on out of town.

When he looked back, he could still see Jack standing in the doorway of the jail.

The sun was hot on Vincent's back as he rode, and he could feel the sweat soaking into his shirt. It was one of the hottest days of the summer so far, and getting hotter all the time.

He was thinking about Jack Simkins, wondering if the deputy was telling the truth, and wondering at the same time why he was doubting him. Jack had never shown any inclination to lie. Why would he begin now?

Of course, Vincent knew the answer to that one. Anybody who would kill would certainly lie, and Jack had never killed before, either, at least as far as Vincent knew.

Vincent knew the story about Jack losing his eye and getting his face so messed up, though it wasn't told around town much anymore. Folks had told it in the past to explain why Jack was a little hesitant when it came to fighting. Now they didn't think about it that much; they just accepted Jack as being that way.

It hadn't happened in Dry Springs. It had happened down close to the border somewhere, and according to the story Jack Simkins had been in a hell of a fight.

Vincent jumped in the saddle a bit as he remembered that the fight had supposedly been over a woman. Jack hadn't killed anybody, though. He'd come close to it, and he'd nearly gotten killed himself, but he hadn't killed anybody. That was Jack's version of the story, anyhow.

There had been a woman named Estrella — "Means 'star,'" Jack had told him one time. "I don't think it was her real name, though. She was sure a pretty woman, and she was workin' in a little cantina down there. She talked to me mighty sweet, which a lot of women did in those days. I didn't look like I do now. Anyhow, I didn't know she was talkin' to two or three other fellas the same way when I wasn't around. I guess she thought they were pretty good-lookin', too."

He had found out about the other men the hard way. One night while he was sitting in the cantina with Estrella on his lap, the other three men had all come in. Seems they'd gotten together in some other bar, drinking and talking, and discovered that they were all in love with women who had the same name. It didn't take them too long to get from there to figuring out that it wasn't different women, that it was the same woman. They decided to confront her and make her choose among them.

So they all came through the door, and there was Jack with the woman on his lap. They had figured three men for one woman was bad enough, and they sure hadn't figured on a fourth. Jack always smiled when he told that part, though it wasn't really very funny.

"All of a sudden they musta decided that they weren't mad at each other anymore, but they were mad as hell at Estrella. And they were damn sure mad at me."

They pulled their guns and started to blaze away. Jack had the woman on his lap and couldn't get her off to get to his gun, but that problem was taken care of when one of the shots from the other men hit her in the side of the head.

"It was an accident, I think," Jack said. "But it was awful bad, all the same. That beautiful face, all that black hair — well, there wasn't hardly anything left of it. Blood splattered all over me. I woulda been sick if I hadn't been so scared."

Estrella fell sideways off his lap, and he managed to get to his pistol. Except for the three men with pistols, everyone else in the place was long gone, out the door, out the windows, or hiding under the bar and the tables. Bullets were flying everywhere, but fortunately the men were so drunk that no one else was hit, not even by accident. They broke the mirror behind the bar and blew a lot of bottles of whiskey all to hell, and even put a couple of holes in the piano.

Jack winged one of the men, knocking him out of the fight, and the other two were out of bullets by then. The fight should have been over, but the men were so mad about having killed the woman that they charged Jack, who got off a couple of shots and missed with both of them.

Then the two men were all over him, hitting him with everything they had, including their pistol barrels and butts. It was a pistol sight ripping down his face that had put the long scar there, and it was a pistol barrel that put his eye out.

"I was doin' my best to keep 'em from killin' me," Jack said, "which they were bound and determined to do, I guess. I got the ear of one of 'em in my teeth and just about got it tore off when he stuck his gun barrel in my eye."

As with the killing of the woman, the eye gouging had apparently been an accident. The man was swinging wildly, trying to do anything to free his ear, and had stuck the pistol barrel in exactly the right spot.

"That eye popped out like it was a grape, slick as you please," Jack said. "Hurt like hell, too, and it hurt even worse when I rolled over and saw it with my good eye. It was lyin' there on the table, lookin' back at me."

The sight had given Jack a strength he didn't know he had. He had kept his teeth on the man's ear and thrown him halfway across the cantina.

"The sound of that ear rippin' off was enough to stop me," he said, "not to mention the blood. You wouldn't think a ear could bleed that much. I spit it on the floor and cold-cocked the other fella with my own pistol. That was the end of it. Lookin' at that ear on the floor and my own eye on the table was enough to make me puke, and there was Estrella lyin' there with the whole side of her head blowed off. I just wanted to get outa there."

He was a little crazy by then, he admitted. "Took my eye off the table and put it in my pocket. Don't know what the hell good I thought it'd do me, but I took it just the same."

He went out of the cantina, and there were men there, the sheriff of the little town and a few of the citizens he'd deputized for the occasion after someone had run to the jail with news of the gun battle that was raging down the street, but for some reason nobody tried to stop him.

"I guess they were scared to," Jack said. "I musta looked like the wrath of God, covered with blood, blood runnin' down my face from where the gun sight raked me and pourin' outa my eye socket. Hell, there was plenty of Estrella's blood on me, too, and prob'ly part of her head. Anyhow, that bunch just split down the middle and I walked right through 'em. There wasn't a one of 'em that didn't stand aside. Nobody even made a move to stop me. Nobody put a hand out."

Jack found his horse and rode away from there that very night, never even stopping for a doctor to see about his eye or the wound on his face.

"Had a bottle of whiskey in my saddlebags," he said. "I used to drink a bit in those days, so I always had a bottle around with me some-where, wrapped up in a saddle blanket so as not to break it."

He stopped a few miles out of town, got out the whiskey, and tied up his horse. Then he lay down under a tree and poured the whis-key in his eye and on his face, after first clean-ing himself up as best he could with his bandanna.

"Burn?" he said. "I guess it did. Not for long, though, 'cause I flat just passed out from the hurtin'. Just as well. I don't never want to feel anything like that again. That's about as near to dyin' as I've ever been, and I don't want to get that near again for a long time. I was all right by the next day, but by the time I remembered that I had my eye in my pocket it was in bad shape. Didn't look anything like a eye, to tell the truth. I pitched it away in a patch of cactus."

After that, Jack drifted around the border for a while, picking up the glass eye along the way, then worked his way north and wound up in Dry Springs. He'd taken the deputy's job because it was something to do and because Ward Vincent had assured him there was no danger in it, despite the way the last sheriff had died.

"Nothin' ever happens here," Vincent said. "Worst scrape you might get into would be some drunk cowboy tryin' to force his affections on some saloon girl that's too tired to fool with him that night. And how often do you think that would happen?"

"Never, prob'ly," Jack said.

"That's right. You do the job right, you'll never have to worry about gettin' shot up or losin' that other eye."

That was just fine by Jack, who admitted

himself, though only to Vincent, that what had happened to him down on the border had changed his outlook on a whole lot of things.

"I don't know what it was," he said. "Whether it was my eye, or bitin' that fella's ear off, or the way Estrella looked lyin' there on the floor. She'd been so pretty before, so happy, tellin' me about how she was gonna leave that cantina someday with a big, good-lookin' fella like me and go off and have a house full of kids and cook and get fat. Then there she was, dead and bloody and ugly, never goin' anywhere again, much less with me."

Things like that happened more often than you'd think in the bars and cantinas, and they bothered lots of people less than they bothered Jack. He was the kind who took the whole episode to heart.

"Seems like I just never had the stomach for killin' after that," he said. "Or even for fightin' much. I can hold down the deputy job, though, if it's as easy as you say."

It was, and Jack had done a good job over the years. There had never been any call for him to engage in violence, and he never had.

So why am I worried about him? Vincent wondered. It was probably because of the old incident, that was all, and there wasn't really any similarity between the two. If Jack hated violence so much, there wasn't any chance he would have killed Liz Randall, and his having no stomach for it probably did more than anything else to explain why he had stood up to the men. He was ashamed of his own part, however small it had been, in what they had done to Paco. Having experienced a similar fate himself, he would naturally want to stand up for the boy.

Wouldn't he? Somehow Vincent couldn't quite stop thinking about it.

And there was something else that was bothering him, something he couldn't quite pin down, that was squirming around in the back of his mind. He thought it was important, but he figured that if it was, it would come clear sooner or later.

He had plenty of other things to worry about right now, more than he wanted, and the first one was how he was going to find Paco Morales.

Chapter Twenty-Two

Len Hawkins handed Harl Case a box of 12-gauge shotgun shells.

"If that don't do the job on him, nothin' will," Hawkins said.

Harl hefted the box in his right hand. In his left he was holding the Whitney single-shot that Len had already given him.

"It won't shoot but once, but if you hit him with it, once will be all you need," Len said. "You can count on that, all right."

Len's store hadn't been opened that day, since Len did all the work himself, but he didn't mind taking a day off in a good cause. Catching up with Paco Morales seemed like a good enough cause to him.

Len was going to take his Winchester repeater, but Harl didn't have anything but a handgun, and that hadn't been fired in years.

"Hell, you can't do this kinda work with some old hogleg that you don't even know'll shoot," Len said. "We'll go over to the store and I'll fix you up right and proper."

Everyone else thought of himself as appropriately armed. The cowboys all had pistols that they considered adequate. Charley Davis and Benteen had rifles, as did Turley Ross. Lane Harper was the only one who didn't carry a weapon as a matter of course, but he said he could take the sawed-off double-barrel that was kept behind the bar at Danton's Saloon.

"If I get close enough to use it, we won't have to worry about diggin' a grave," he said. "There won't be enough of that Meskin left to bury." Everybody knew it was pretty much the truth. You could blow off a barn door and kill a horse with the same shot from a sawed-off.

Harl looked around the store. In the dim light he could see the barrels of nails, the bundles of ax handles and hoe handles, the plowshares, the pistols behind the glass of the counter. It might have been his imagination, but he thought he could smell gun oil.

"Better put you a shell in the breech," Len told him. "You don't want to get caught off guard."

Harl was wondering about that. How was he going to get caught off guard by a kid? How come they needed so many men to go after him? It wasn't like they were going after Wes Hardin or Jesse James.

When it came right down to it, Harl was having second thoughts about the whole thing. He wasn't a gunman by either inclination or practice. He liked animals, and he liked taking care of them. Did a good job of it, too, according to all his customers.

He had kept the livery stable for fifteen years in Dry Springs. For the last couple of years, his boys had been old enough to do most of the work, and he'd more or less turned it over to them. That was why he had time to have a few drinks now and then. It was why he'd been in the saloon at least two different times when he wished to hell he'd been somewhere else.

The first time had been when the elder Morales had been killed.

The second was last night, when that Jack Simkins had come by, asking if they could go looking for the preacher's girl. How did he get into things like that, anyhow? Maybe he ought to start spending more time at home and a lot less around places that sold liquor.

He slipped a 12-gauge shell into the breech of the Whitney and looked at Len. "You reckon we're doin' the right thing?" he asked.

"What the hell does that mean?" Hawkins asked. He was feeding shells into the Winchester. "We're goin' after a killer. That's the right thing, ain't it?"

Harl shrugged. "Maybe not; it all depends."

Len laid the rifle down on the countertop. "You beginnin' to turn yellow, Harl? I wouldn't've thought it of you."

Harl shook his head. "It ain't that. I ain't afraid. But the truth of the matter is, we ain't really got no business goin' after that boy. We got us a sheriff in town for that kind of thing. Maybe we oughta leave it to him. It's his job to do, after all."

"You know Ward Vincent as well as I do," Len said. "He's a good enough fella, steady. You can depend on him to be there when there's a drunk needs throwed out of the saloon on Saturday night or when somebody steals a cow — which ain't happened in years, now that I think of it. Comes to somethin' like this, though, well, he's a little skittish. You remember when that gambler shot that Meskin?"

"Paco's daddy," Harl said. "Sure, I remember. I wish I didn't."

"Well, that's the kinda thing I mean," Len said. "You and me both know what happened that time, and if Vincent had pushed it, he would've found out. He didn't though."

"Nobody wanted him to," Harl pointed out. He was thinking about the way it had happened that time. He had figured that Moran was cheating, just like Morales had, but he

192

hadn't wanted to call him on it. There was something about the gambler's eyes that Harl didn't like, something that said trouble just as plain as if Moran had a sign hanging around his neck. Besides, he couldn't figure out just how the cheating was done.

Morales hadn't figured it out, either, but he'd finally had enough. When he'd called Moran a cheater, the gambler hadn't hesitated. He'd pulled his big pistol and shot Morales right in the chest.

"You all saw what happened, didn't you?" Moran said.

Most of them had hesitated to say they had, but Moran still had his gun in his hand, so finally somebody — it was Turley Ross, Harl thought, or maybe Lane Harper — said, "Yeah. We saw it. He made the first move."

After that, they all went along. Morales was just a Meskin anyhow, and Moran had a right to shoot somebody that was calling him a cheat, if the fella couldn't prove it. Even Harl went along, though he hadn't really felt right about it. He wondered what would've happened if he'd been the one to say something about the cheating. If it had been him that got shot, how long would it've taken his buddies to say the same thing they were saying about Morales?

He even wondered how long it would've

taken him to say the same thing about them.

Moran had been icy calm about the shooting. When he saw that things were going his way, he holstered the pistol and said, "These damn greasers ought never to gamble. They don't know anything about how to play cards, and they always try to say an honest man is cheatin' when they don't win. I reckon that's the reason he went for his knife. We ought never to've let him get into the game."

He was right about letting Morales have a seat at the table, and Harl knew it as well as anybody. They usually didn't let Meskins in any of the games in the saloon. It was all right for them to have a drink or two, but letting 'em in a game was just asking for trouble.

Still, Morales seemed like a steady sort. He'd lived around town for as long as anybody could remember, had a nice family, kept more or less to himself, and never bothered anybody. He had a little money, and there didn't seem to be any harm in letting him sit in for a few hands. He'd done it before, but there hadn't been any outsiders playing at the time.

And what was that business about a knife? Morales didn't have any knife, not that Harl could remember ever seeing.

That is, he didn't have one the first time Harl looked at him lying there on the floor with the blood soaking into the front of his shirt.

He sure as hell did the next time Harl looked, though. A real pig-sticker, lying right there by his right hand like he'd dropped it when he fell.

Now where did that come from? Harl thought.

Well, he knew where. The gambler, when he'd put his gun up, had reached into his boot and come out with something and put it by the body. Harl hadn't really been looking. But it was the knife that he'd put there, no question about it.

"These Meskins really like knives," Moran said to no one in particular. "Prob'ly had it in his boot. That's where they carry 'em, mostly."

"That's the truth," somebody said. "They all got one they carry there."

It didn't matter who said that. Harl couldn't remember. But he knew it was a lie, even at the time. Nobody in that saloon could remember ever seeing Morales with a knife.

They all went along with the lie, though, and it seemed to Harl like a sorry coincidence that the same bunch had to be in the saloon to be called out to look for the Randall girl and to find Morales's boy there with her body. Since they were the usual steady customers in Danton's, it wasn't much of a coincidence, really, but it was a shame anyhow.

Harl tried to think who else had been there at the card game, but he couldn't think of anybody except for Willie Turner, and Turner had been too drunk to notice anything. At least that's what everybody thought. Anyhow, he'd never said anything about what happened.

What happened was that they'd all taken the easiest way out, Harl thought. They'd let a man get away with murder because they didn't have the gumption to stand up to him. Maybe they were afraid of getting hurt, or maybe they were afraid to take the side of a dead Meskin against another white man. For whatever reason, they'd gone along.

And now Harl was afraid they were doing it again. He was just a man who liked horses and had a livery stable. He'd never hurt anybody on purpose, never even gotten into a fight in his life. Now here he was, standing with a scatter gun in his hands, about to go gunning for a boy — just a kid.

What if they were wrong about it? They'd had a little to drink last night, and when they saw Paco Morales, they'd gotten a little carried away. Nothing wrong with that. They'd seen that girl, and Lordy she was cut up. No wonder things got a little out of hand when they saw Paco. Maybe they were wrong to do it, but nobody could blame them for that, and they could make up for it now. It wasn't too late.

"Len," he said, "what if that boy didn't do it?"

"He did it," Len said, picking up his rifle. "We saw him."

"We saw him there in the grove. We didn't see him lay a hand on that girl any more than we saw his daddy pull a knife on that gambler."

"Talkin' that way won't do no good," Len said. "Let's get on back before they leave without us."

He walked by Harl and over to the door. "Come on. I ain't gonna wait for you all day."

Standing there in the doorway, the light behind him, he looked to Harl like a skeleton with a rifle dangling from its bony hand. That's how skinny he was.

"Len, what if someday it comes out about how there wasn't no knife that other time and the sheriff finds out that it was all Moran's fault that Morales got killed?"

"Who's gonna tell him? You?"

"No. No, I never meant anything like that."

"It's a good thing. Ain't nobody gonna tell, and that sheriff ain't gonna find out any other way. Now, are you comin' or not."

"I'm comin'," Harl said.

Chapter Twenty-Three

Benteen drew Charley to a table in a corner of the saloon. He had a few things he wanted to say before they left. It wouldn't hurt to let everyone have a few more drinks; liquor was just the thing to get them in the mood for what they were about to do. Benteen himself was not a drinking man, but he understood the appeal it had for others.

"I want to talk to you a minute," he told Charley when they were seated. "What's this about the sheriff calming Lucille down?"

"She was a little upset with me," Charley explained. "She was doin' a little shootin'."

Benteen nodded. His daughter was a strong-willed, hot-tempered woman, and she knew how to handle a gun. "She have a reason to be doing that?"

"Not a bit of one," Charley said, looking Benteen straight in the eye. "I didn't have anything to do with that girl gettin' herself killed."

"I want to believe that," Benteen said, his

glance not wavering from Charley's. "It had better be the truth."

"It is," Charley said, hoping the old man couldn't read his mind and wishing he'd never gone out of the bunkhouse last night. There were men right there in the room who knew he hadn't gotten there till late, but they hadn't said anything yet. Maybe they wouldn't, ever. You never could tell when they might, though.

"You're sweating a lot, Charley," Benteen said. "You sure you're telling me everything?"

"It's a hot day," Charley said. He could feel the sweat running down the back of his neck. "I hadn't been seein' Liz for more'n a month, and that's God's truth."

"Very well," Benteen said. "And God help you if it isn't. Let's see if we can get this little party started."

He moved his chair back from the table and got up. Charley watched his straight back as he walked to the men at the bar. Then he glanced around at one of the other tables and saw the preacher looking at him. The preacher's eyes were like holes in a skull. The sweat on Charley's body felt suddenly chilled.

Lucille Benteen saw the men leave the saloon, her father and Charley among them. She heard them, too, yelling and calling out to each other as they stumbled around. They mounted up and swirled away in a cloud of dust, but for some reason they were not headed for the ranch. She wondered where they could be going. It wasn't like her father to go off like that, without coming back by to tell her what he had said to Charley or what Charley had said to him. And the preacher was with them. What on earth would they be doing with the preacher? Her father hadn't been to church in years.

As the last of the riders passed down the street, another man came out of the saloon door and stood watching them. He looked familiar to Lucille, and she realized that he was Willie Turner. She remembered how he had lost his family and taken to drinking. He looked sober enough now, however. She decided to satisfy her curiosity by asking him what was going on.

She went downstairs and through the lobby. The desk clerk looked up as she passed, but he didn't say anything. She was a very attractive woman, he thought, and he admired the way her riding britches fit, but she sure was a hellcat. He would've hated to be that Charley Davis and have her mad at him.

When Lucille got outside, Willie Turner was still standing on the boardwalk under the saloon awning, though the riders were by now nearly out of sight. Lucille crossed over to him, looking up and down the street as she did so. There were very few people out in the heat of the day. A woman with a parasol was going in the dry-goods store, and one wagon moved slowly past. Two lank dogs were barking as they chased a cat down the street and into an alley, but they didn't look or sound particularly enthusiastic about it.

Lucille stepped up on the boardwalk beside Willie. "Mr. Turner?" she said.

Willie turned to look at her. He hadn't shaved in a good while, and he was unpleasantly fragrant, but Lucille was used to cowhands who didn't bathe much more often than Willie. She was not offended.

"Who're you?" Willie said.

"I'm Lucille Benteen, Roger Benteen's daughter."

"Oh," Willie said vaguely. "I guess I should've known that. Seems like I can't remember too good anymore, though."

"I was wondering," Lucille said, "where is everyone going?"

"The Morales place," Willie said.

"What are they going out there for?"

"You ain't heard?"

"Heard what?"

"About Liz Randall."

"No. What about her?"

Willie was reluctant to tell the story, but at

the same time he found himself wanting to tell, and it all came spilling out, even the part about how he knew that what they were doing was wrong.

Lucille was horrified by the story, especially by what had happened to Liz. She had nothing against the girl; she blamed Charley entirely for whatever had been going on between them, and it was terrible to think that a killer could be lurking around Dry Springs. But what Willie seemed to be saying now was even more horrifying.

"What do you mean they're doing the wrong thing? What are they going to do?"

"I think they want to hang that boy," Willie said. "And he didn't have anything to do with killin' Liz Randall."

"How do you know that?" Lucille said.

Willie's face twisted as if he were in pain. "I don't *know* how I know it. I just do. It seems like I was I *there,* like there's somethin' I oughta know, but that I just can't think of somehow."

"Did . . . did you kill her?" Lucille asked.

"That's the worst part," Willie said. "I don't think I did, but I can't swear I didn't."

"And you let them go after that boy? What kind of a man are you?"

"The kind that thinks too much of his own worthless hide," Willie said. "I know how that prob'ly sounds to you. It sounds the same to me. I know how worthless I am, and I've thought more than once that I oughta kill myself to put myself out of my misery, but I've never had the guts to do it. Maybe I shoulda told 'em that I was the one. That way they'd've had somebody to kill and I —"

"Don't be stupid," Lucille said. Her sense of justice was aroused. "Try to think about last night. Did you see that Randall girl? Did you see what happened to her?"

Willie put both hands to his head and wagged it from side to side. "I don't know," he said. "I don't know. I don't know."

"Stop it!" Lucille said. She did not have much patience with self-pitying drunks. "You must know something, or you wouldn't be acting this way. Now try to think."

Willie shut up and tried to think. He could remember seeing Liz's body, and he could remember seeing the Morales boy, but not both at the same time. He could remember —

"That's it!" he said. "I was stumbling around, and that boy come up on the body. He got scared and started in to runnin', and I went after him, to tell him it was all right, but he just started to run faster. Then I got scared. I thought, what if somebody came along and found me there? So I left. I thought the boy'd gone on home until this mornin', when I heard 'em talkin' in the saloon."

Lucille tried to make sense of what he had told her. "So you were there before the boy was?"

"Yeah, that's right," Willie said. More of it was coming back to him now. "He was comin' along from town, and I hid in the brush so he wouldn't see me. I thought he'd go right on by, but he didn't."

Lucille was exasperated with him. "And knowing all that, you let those men go after him?"

Willie could not meet her eyes. "I didn't know all that. I didn't remember it till just now."

"You knew the boy was innocent all along," she accused him.

"I thought he was, but I couldn't say so. Nobody'd listen to an old drunk."

"What is my father doing mixed up in this?" Lucille said.

"I don't know," Willie said. "That Davis fella came in tellin' about the boy's mama lettin' him out, and then your daddy came. I guess they just thought goin' after him was the right thing to do."

There was more to it than that, Lucille thought, though she was not sure exactly what.

"We've got to stop them," she said.

"Stop 'em? How're we gonna do that?"

"We're going after them."

"But I don't have any horse." Willie had sold his horse along with everything else. He hadn't had occasion to ride for years.

"Let me worry about that. Come on." Lucille grabbed his arm. "We'll go down to the livery. My horse is there, and I'll get you one."

Willie tried to pull his arm away. "I don't think that's a good idea. They won't listen to me. You don't know how they are. They're all worked up to get somebody, and they don't want any interference."

Lucille wasn't going to let that stop her. "I don't care what they want. We're going to stop them."

Willie thought she was wrong about that, but he couldn't get his arm out of her grip. She was damn strong for a girl, he thought. She half dragged him all the way to the livery stable.

"It won't do any good," he protested along the way. "Besides, they might decide to kill me if they don't get their chance at the boy."

"Why would they do that?" Lucille asked.

"Because I was there. They might think I —"

Lucille stopped in her tracks. "You said you didn't kill her. Now make up your mind. Did you or didn't you?"

"No," Willie said. "I didn't kill her." He

looked thoughtful. "At least I don't think I killed her."

Lucille was exasperated. "Don't you even know whether you killed her or not?"

"No," Willie said. "I don't guess I do."

Chapter Twenty-Four

Jack Simkins heard the men ride past the jail. He got up from the chair behind the desk and walked slowly over to the door, reaching it just in time to see the last of Benteen's riders go by. Turley Ross and the other men from the saloon were right behind, but they didn't even give a look in Jack's direction as they rode on down the street.

Jack had a pretty good idea where they were going, all right, but the sheriff had ordered him to stay in the jail and that's what he was going to do. He had never yet failed to do anything the sheriff told him to do, and he wasn't going to start now.

There was a little breeze blowing, and Jack thought it would be a good idea to bring his chair out on the porch. There was a spot of shade that he could set it in, and it would be somewhat cooler out there than in the stuffy office. He got the chair, brought it out, sat down in it, and tipped it back against the wall, hooking his boot heels on the rung that ran between the two front legs. He slanted his hat down over his eyes and had almost drifted off to sleep when he heard someone calling him.

He brought the chair down with a thump that jarred his spine and pulled his hat off to see who was talking. It was Willie Turner and Lucille Benteen.

Now there was a pair for you, he thought, getting out of the chair and standing up. "Howdy," he said. "What can I do for you?"

"Where's the sheriff?" Lucille said. She did not have much confidence in either man, but she thought that Vincent had more sand than his deputy.

"He's off on official sheriff's business," Jack said. He didn't like the young woman's tone of voice. "You can tell me what you want, and I'll let him know."

"We want to talk to him about that bunch of riders that went by here awhile ago," Lucille said. "They're headed for the Morales place, and they might have the idea that they're going to lynch the Morales boy."

"The sheriff, he might have other ideas about that. He's headed that way himself," Jack said. "What's all this to you, anyhow?"

"I don't like to see an innocent boy killed, that's what, and if you had any decency, you'd feel the same."

"Now you just wait a minute," Jack said.

"How do you know he's so all-fired innocent?"

"Mr. Turner told me."

"Mr. Turner?" Jack looked at Willie skeptically. "What's your part in all this, Willie?"

Willie didn't say anything, so Lucille answered for him.

"He was there last night. He saw what happened."

"Is that right, Willie?" Jack said. "You were there?"

Willie nodded, but he still didn't say anything.

"What did you see, Willie?" Jack said.

"N-N-Nothin'," Willie said. "I didn't see nothin'."

"That's not what you told me," Lucille said. "Tell him the truth."

"I saw that Morales boy," Willie said.

Lucille was disgusted with Willie's performance. "You're only making things worse. Tell him what you told me, and don't worry so much about your own skin."

Willie was ashamed of himself for being such a coward, but he couldn't help it. He didn't want to die, not even if he deserved it. All these years since he'd lost his wife and little girl, he'd thought he wanted to die himself. Now he knew that wasn't so. He wanted to keep on living, even if it meant living like a drunk.

"Like I said, I saw the Morales boy there. But he didn't kill that girl. He didn't come along till she'd been dead awhile."

"How do you know that?" Jack asked. He seemed more interested now. "Did you see who killed her?"

"I . . . I don't think so," Willie said. "I can't remember that part so good."

"But you're sure it wasn't the Morales kid."

"Yeah," Willie said. "I'm sure of that."

"Would you be willing to testify to that in court?"

Willie shook his head. "I don't know about that, now."

"Of course he would," Lucille said. "Now what are you going to do about this?"

"Like I said, the sheriff is on his way out there now. That gang'll run into him before they get there, most likely."

"Do you think one man's going to be able to stop them?" Lucille asked. Especially the sheriff, she thought. He couldn't stop a lame hog. "I'm going after them, and if you were any kind of a lawman, you'd come, too."

"The sheriff told me to stay here and watch the jail," Jack said.

"How much good is that going to do the sheriff if he's dead?" Lucille asked. "Well, never mind. We don't need your help."

"Yes, we do," Willie said. "Come on, Jack.

Don't make us do this by ourselves. The sheriff won't mind. Not just this one time."

"I guess maybe he wouldn't," Jack said. He was thinking about all those men he had seen. There had been a lot of them. The sheriff wouldn't stand a chance if they didn't listen to reason. Maybe another gun would help, but he didn't see that a drunk, a woman, and a one-eyed deputy would do all that much good.

However, he also remembered what had happened to Paco last night. If Jack hadn't been there, they would have killed the boy right on the spot. Maybe that was what they had in mind to do this time; only this time there were a lot more of them.

He looked at his chair and his little spot of shade. He wished he'd never brought that chair out there; if he'd been inside, maybe they'd've ridden right on by and not bothered him.

Then again, maybe they wouldn't've.

"I'm comin'," he said. "Just let me get my rifle."

Like Jack Simkins and Willie Turner, Charley Davis was wondering how he'd ever gotten himself into this mess.

He'd started courting Liz Randall because she was just about the prettiest girl in Dry Springs, if you didn't count Lucille, and the fact that they had to sneak around about it didn't bother him. He never dreamed he would have a chance with Lucille, and Liz Randall wasn't like any other girl he'd ever known.

She was a "nice" girl, the preacher's daughter, and Charley had associated mostly with women he met in saloons, many of whom were interested in sex mainly for the money or else were there because there wasn't much chance of them finding a man any other place. They were counting on finding them somebody who'd had so much bad liquor to drink that even a range cow would've looked good to him.

Liz Randall, on the other hand, had been interested in sex because she liked it, and while Charley had thought at first he would be teaching her a trick or two, he soon found out that he was going to be more like the student than the teacher.

That was all right with him for a while, but eventually she began to scare him a little. It somehow didn't seem right to him that a woman ought to talk the way she did and make the kind of demands she made.

A woman ought to have a little modesty, but she'd just as soon shuck out of her clothes right in front of him as not.

At first that had been fine. It even excited

him. At first he had been so caught up in the sight of her, the fine round breasts, the red hair between her legs like spun gold, the light sprinkling of freckles across her belly, that whatever she did was all right with him. He'd never had a woman who could make him feel the way she did.

But after that, things changed.

Or maybe they didn't change at all. Charley had to admit that maybe he was the one who changed. But some of the things Liz did began to bother him, like the way she'd just reach out and grab him down there sometimes without warning, or the way she was getting bolder about being seen with him.

"I thought you didn't want your daddy to know about us," he said. "You didn't want anybody to know you were even out of the house."

Liz laughed. "My daddy's a crazy man. He treats me like I was still a little girl, and it's time he knew I was all grown up. He'll know, all right, soon enough."

She hadn't explained what she meant that time, and Charley hadn't pushed it. By then he had already become involved with Lucille Benteen.

Lucille was a lot different from Liz, more mature, he guessed, but he liked her a lot. Besides, she was Roger Benteen's girl, and if the old man liked Charley, well, there was no telling what might come of it.

The old man did like Charley, as it turned out, and Charley began to see Lucille more and more and Liz less and less.

The night he told Liz he couldn't be seeing her anymore was when she told him.

"I'm going to have a baby, Charley. Your baby."

Charley didn't doubt that she was telling the truth, especially considering what they'd been doing together, but he said, "You sure?"

"Of course I'm sure. But you don't have to believe me. Ask Doc Bigby. Ask Mrs. Morales. They know."

Charley was hard put to know what to do, but he'd heard things. "Ain't there something they can do about it?"

"No. I asked them both, believe me. I don't want to have any baby. I thought at first I might, that it would be a good lesson for my father, but now I know it would be a big mistake. My father's already crazy. No telling what me having a baby would do to him."

"But there's gotta be somethin' —"

"We could get married," Liz said. She didn't sound too happy about the idea, though.

"Is that what you want to do?" Charley hoped she didn't. He couldn't let himself get caught in that trap, not when he was doing so well with Lucille. Liz was all right, it wasn't that, but she didn't have much to offer compared to Roger Benteen's ranch.

"No, I don't want to do it," Liz said. "But we might have to. I don't want to have a baby with no father."

Charley talked to her for a long time. He finally persuaded her to go back to the Meskin woman to see if there was anything that she could do if Charley paid her. Liz didn't have much money, and Charley thought maybe if they offered more the woman would change her mind.

"I'll try," Liz said. "I don't hold out much hope of her doing anything, I may as well tell you."

Charley gave her some money and told her to do what she could. He agonized for a week about it, hardly sleeping at all, not being able to eat, getting as jumpy as some old cat. He was sure people had noticed, but nobody ever said anything, not even Lucille until right there at the last, after somebody told her that he'd been seeing Liz.

"Now I know why you've been acting funny," Lucille said. "You think you can have me and some other woman, too. Well, you can't."

She'd slapped his face and ridden off to town, and of course he'd gone after her with his tail between his legs. Now here he was, off to hang some poor Meskin kid for killin' Liz.

He hadn't seen the kid last night, but he'd seen Liz. He was there to find out what she'd learned about her condition. It hadn't been good.

"It's too late," she said. "Even if there'd been something they could have done sooner, it's too late now. I'm going to have the baby. I've got to."

Well, she was wrong about that, as it turned out, Charley thought. She wasn't ever going to have the baby now, and he was beginning to wonder if he was ever going to marry Lucille Benteen. Maybe it had been too much to hope for in the first place. Maybe he should've been happy just to wrangle horses and punch cows.

He looked around at the other cowboys as they rode, laughing and talking about what they were going to do to Paco Morales. They were happy, he thought, and they weren't ever going to marry the boss's daughter. Why couldn't he have been satisfied?

If he had been, maybe Liz would still be alive and maybe Paco Morales wouldn't be about to die.

It was too bad that things worked out like they did sometimes, but that was just the way it was. He didn't have anything against the

Morales boy, but he had to think about himself. If somebody had to die, it might as well be the Meskin.

He sneaked another look at Randall, sitting rigid in the saddle, his hard belly sticking out past the sides of his black coat, his eyes staring straight ahead, his hand never far from the butt of the pistol on his hip.

It was scary to see a preacher like that, real scary, and Charley looked away quick, but not before the preacher caught him looking and smiled at him.

It was a smile Charley wished he hadn't seen, like seeing a dead man smile.

Charley didn't smile back.

Chapter Twenty-Five

The Morales place looked deserted. There were a few scrawny rust-colored chickens pecking in the dirt around on the shady side of the house, and there was a dog sleeping under the porch. Aside from that, there wasn't any sign of life.

Sheriff Vincent stopped his horse a few yards from the front door. "Hello," he called out, standing up in the stirrups.

The dog lifted its head from its paws, opened its eyes, and looked at him incuriously. It scratched its neck with its back leg and then settled back down to sleep again. There was no answer from the house.

"Now then, Miz Morales, I know you're there," Vincent said. "You might's well come out here and talk to me."

The front door opened, and Consuela Morales stepped out on the porch. The dog pricked up its ears for a second, but not for long.

"Yes, Sheriff?" she said.

218

"I've come for your boy," Vincent said, settling himself back in the saddle. "It was because of my carelessness he got out of the jail, and I don't blame you for it, but you know I've got to take him back."

"He is not here," Mrs. Morales said. "As you can see."

"I can't see anything like that," Vincent said. "I don't know what's in your house."

"You may look if it pleases you, but you will not find my son. He was here, it is true, but he is gone now. He took the mule and rode away."

"I don't think so," Vincent said, shifting his weight in the saddle. "He wasn't in any shape to do much ridin' when I last saw him."

He looked around, but he didn't see the mule. He wished that the woman wouldn't give him any more trouble. He was having enough trouble already, what with Charley Davis admitting to having seen the girl and with that bunch from the saloon wanting to take Paco out of the jail and do no telling what to the boy, not to mention the preacher's wife saying that maybe her husband had killed his own daughter, and with even Jack admitting to having known more than he should've about Liz Randall.

"He'd be better off if he came with me," Vincent said. "I can have the doc in to look at him, and I can keep him safe till the trial."

"There was no trial for my husband's killer," she said. "You did not keep my husband safe."

Vincent wished she wouldn't bring that up. He felt bad about that, but there hadn't been anything he could do about it. He hadn't even been there when the man got shot.

"Nobody's going to hurt your son," he said, hoping that he was telling the truth. This time there was a lot of evidence to indicate that even if Paco had been caught in a pretty bad situation, there were others who shared that situation with him. Vincent didn't know how much good that evidence would do Paco, however.

"That is what you say. It may even be what you wish. But it is not what others might wish."

Hell, what could he say to that? She was right.

"I'll do my best by him," he said finally. It was all that he could say, and even saying that much caused him a twinge and brought a bad taste into his mouth. He didn't want to have to stand up to anybody to save the boy's life. He didn't want to have to stand up to anybody for anything.

"Anyway, he is not here," Mrs. Morales said. "You may search the house now if you wish, but you will not find him there."

Vincent slid off the horse. The dog perked up again, and the chickens left off their pecking to look at him.

"I guess I'll just have to take a look, anyhow," he said. He had a sinking feeling that she was telling the truth, however. He wondered where the hell the boy had got to.

In the shed Paco heard the whole conversation. It was almost as if his mother and the sheriff were discussing someone else, a person that Paco was not even related to, but at the same time he knew what was happening. He felt light-headed and dreamy, and he wondered if he had a fever or if he was coming close to suffocation in the almost airless shed. He tightened his grip on the rifle, the smooth stock slippery under his sweaty hands.

He hoped the sheriff would look in the house and then leave. He did not want to kill the sheriff.

He would do it, though. He would not go back to the jail, where he knew that sooner or later he would die for killing the girl. The fact that he was innocent would not save him. No one would care about that.

If the sheriff opened the shed door, then Paco would have no choice.

The house wasn't much, and Vincent didn't find the boy. He found the two little girls, and he found two sparsely furnished bed-rooms, a kitchen with a dingy stove and a rickety wood table and four chairs, and a sitting room that had a couple of chairs and a raggedy settee in it, but that was all.

"You see," Consuela Morales said. "He is not here."

"He ain't in the house," Vincent agreed. "He's around here somewhere, though."

"No," Consuela said. "He is not here. I told you. He took the mule, and he is gone."

"Yeah, that's what you said." Vincent went past her and out on the porch. He looked around the yard, but it was something off down the road that caught his eye. Looked like riders. He shaded his eyes with his hand.

It was riders, all right, and there wasn't much doubt where they were headed. Vincent fought a sudden urge to get on his horse and get out of there. He was pretty sure he knew what was coming, and he didn't know how to deal with it. Damn those fellas anyhow. Why couldn't they have just stuck to their drinking? He'd heard stories about how one man faced down a mob, but he didn't think he was that kind of man. He didn't like the idea of having to find out, either.

He turned back inside. "Miz Morales, if you know where your boy is, you better tell me right now. There's some more men comin', and they won't be as easy about this as I am."

"I will tell them as I have told you," she said. "He is not here."

"Yeah," Vincent said. "And they won't believe you any more than I do. What's gonna happen then?"

"We will see," she said.

Turley Ross was riding along in front, thinking of how he'd led the men last night and how he was leading them now. He'd never been in charge of anything before, but last night the men had been looking to him for advice, and he'd given it to them. If it hadn't been for that goddamn deputy, they'd've strung that kid up and that would've been the end of it. And everybody would've known that Turley Ross had been the one to get it done. Today, by God, they'd do it right.

It had felt good last night to be the one who knew what to do, the one who was sure of what should be done. He could almost feel the hesitation in the others, even in Len Hawkins and Lane Harper. But Turley Ross didn't hesitate. "Let's string him up here and now," was what he said, and the others all respected him for saying it.

Now he was leading them again, and even Roger Benteen was having to eat his dust.

Thinking about Benteen upset Ross just a

little. He didn't like it that the rancher and his men had dealt themselves in. The preacher, he had a right, and maybe even the gambler did, seeing as how the Morales boy was involved.

Remembering the way Moran had killed the boy's father did not cause Ross even a moment's unrest. Morales was an uppity Meskin, always coming into the saloon and behaving just like he was a white man and had a right. It was just like him to want to sit in on the card game, and what he got was just exactly what he deserved. Turley always kinda wished he could've been the one to have killed him. People would've looked up to him for that.

No one had ever had to look up to Turley before. He was too short for that, and when he'd been a kid all the other boys had picked on him, especially the older ones, the ones that could reach down and pat him on the head. They thought that was so damn smart, patting him on the head like he was some kinda little dog.

They called him names, too, because of the way he looked, with his long arms and stocky build and the way he sort of hunched over when he walked. Somebody saw a picture of a monkey in a book and showed it to all the others. "Turley looks like a monkey," they all said after that.

"Turley the monkey, Turley the monkey," they would yell in their high kids' voices, and then they'd chase after him and try to pat him on the head. Sometimes he thought he could still hear them yelling.

"Nice monkey," they'd say when they caught him. "Nice monkey." And then they'd pat him.

It didn't last for long, though. One evening one of the kids, the one who'd found the picture in the book and showed it around, was walking back to the house from a trip to the privy. Someone came up behind him and hit him with an axe handle. Six or seven times. Broke one of his arms and a couple of ribs and knocked out most of his teeth.

The kid didn't see who did it, never got a chance to. He was too busy trying to cover himself and keep from getting his head broken open.

He knew who it was, though, and so did everyone else, but there was no way they could prove it.

After that, they left Turley alone, strictly alone.

He found out then that there were some things just as bad as being called names and being made fun of. It was hard for a kid not to have any friends at all, not to have anyone to talk to or to go fishing with or anything at all.

Turley got used to it eventually, but he was glad when his folks moved away from that town and he got a chance to start over. He made a few friends, but from that time on he never really trusted anyone. He never knew when they might get behind his back and laugh about him, about the way he looked or the way he walked.

All he wanted was for people to see the good things about him and how he was smarter than most people and knew things about how things worked; he wanted people to look up to him.

Seems like they never did, though. As he got older, he developed a knack for fixing things that were broken. He was good with his hands and a hammer and became a good carpenter and fence builder. His skills were in demand, but still it seemed that no one really respected him.

He got to spending more and more time in the saloon. At least people there talked to him like he was as good as they were, which he certainly was. He was there because he wanted to be, not because he depended on liquor to give him any feeling of self-worth, like he suspected most of them did.

But now he was blossoming like a flower on the prairie. He was showing them that he was a man who could lead, who knew how to handle things.

They were listening to him because they could see that he was right about the Morales boy. They had caught him in the act, raping and killing a white woman, and he had to pay the price for that. Turley couldn't let anybody back down. If that happened, folks might wonder why they'd beat the boy up so bad in the first place — he might even get the judge on his side by telling him some story about how the men who caught him broke his arm or something along that line. The judge might even think they didn't have a right to do that. You never could tell.

So it wouldn't ever come to a trial. Turley Ross would see to that, and later on people would thank him for it. You bet they would.

Chapter Twenty-Six

Moran just wanted to get it over with.

Hell, he didn't care about the kid or the girl he was supposed to have killed. They weren't anything to him. What he wanted was to get back to town and start up a poker game while everybody was feeling good about going out and getting revenge on a kid that probably couldn't even fight back. They'd all be talking big and drinking plenty. That was the kind of men Moran liked to have playing in any game he was part of. The more they talked, the more they drank; and the more they drank and talked, the worse they handled the cards.

Moran hoped they didn't take too long with the kid. It was hot, and he wasn't used to being out in the heat like this. He spent most of his time indoors, and his white skin showed it. He was wearing a pair of soft riding gloves to protect his hands, and his hat would take care of his face, but he still didn't think much of the outdoors, not in the daylight at least.

He looked over at the preacher. There was

another one who wasn't what he seemed to be, but Moran couldn't make out exactly what he was. He sat there in the saddle stiff as a board, mumbling to himself.

That was a bad sign, sure enough. Moran had sat in a game or two with men like that, and they were always impossible to predict. They might play a steady game for a while and then just jump up right in the middle of a hand, kick over the table, and scatter money all over the room. Or they might jerk out a gun and start shooting.

He had seen that happen once, and he had been forced to kill the man. Bastard was hard to put down, took three shots right in the chest and was still standing. Moran put his fourth shot right in the middle of the man's forehead, and he even stood there for a second or two after that, with the back of his head blown clean away. Moran would never forget the look in the man's eyes, like he knew he was dead but didn't want to admit it. Kinda the way the preacher's eyes looked right now, come to think of it.

Moran had gotten out of that little scrape, too, just like he had with the Mex in Dry Springs. Self-defense. That time he hadn't even had to bother planting a weapon so the citizens could feel justified in what they were saying. The man had tried to kill a few of them, too, at one time or another.

"Pure-dee crazy, that was old Jackson," somebody said, which Moran figured was about as much of an epitaph as old Jackson would get and probably more than he deserved.

Now they needed to put the kid down, or hang him on the closest tree. Hell, it was time to play cards.

The closer they got to the Morales place, the less Roger Benteen liked what they were doing.

He had sort of gotten caught up in things, he thought, and that wasn't like him at all. He liked to be in control, and in this case he clearly was not. Things were happening around him that he couldn't seem to do anything about.

First his daughter had run off. As far back as he could remember, she had never done anything like that. She was an independent little cuss, even as a child, but she more or less obeyed him in everything and tried to please him.

And that damn Charley. Benteen couldn't blame the man for getting involved with Liz Randall, but he should have dropped her immediately when Lucille got interested in him. It was hard to get shed of women, though.

Benteen knew that. That was probably one of the reasons why he didn't have anything to do with them.

It was also one of the reasons why he didn't understand the passion that must have been involved in the murder of Liz Randall. Why anyone would want to cut someone up like they told him the girl had been was beyond Benteen's comprehension, and to believe that a fifteen-year-old boy might have done it was almost impossible.

Benteen wondered how he had allowed himself to get caught up in the rush to find Paco Morales and punish him. He guessed it was all the talking and all the excitement, Charley telling him what had happened, the men in the saloon confirming it, all of them making it sound as if Paco was guilty beyond the shadow of a doubt.

Of course, he had to admit as well that his wanting to prove that Charley was free of any recent interest in Liz Randall had a lot to do with it, too, sort of helping him get a handle on things again, but this was just a boy that they were riding against.

It had been a long time since Benteen had ridden against anyone, though at one time or another he had been involved in his share of minor skirmishes over things like fences or water rights or strayed cows.

Never over anything like a woman, however, no matter how she had died, and the whole thing made him vaguely uneasy.

He supposed it was too late to back out now, though. His ranch hands wouldn't understand. They might take it for a sign of weakness, and while that wouldn't make much difference to them, since they would keep on working for the man who paid their wages, it would make a difference to Benteen. He wasn't the kind of man who liked to show weakness.

It was like a big rock that started rolling downhill, he thought. You could stop it if you caught it right at first, but if you waited too long the rock would just go faster and faster. If you stepped in front of it after it got to going, it would just roll right over you and keep on bumping along, leaving you smashed flatter than a pancake behind it.

It was too late to stop this bunch now. They were already too far down the hill and going too damn fast. All he could do was watch what happened and try to stay out of the way and keep from getting flattened. Then he would get everything straightened out between Charley and Lucille, and things would be all right again.

He kept telling himself that as he rode, but somehow he couldn't quite make himself believe it.

The riders pulled up in front of the Morales house, but the big dust cloud they had stirred up kept on going. It rolled across the front yard and onto the porch. A good bit of it settled on Vincent, and he coughed it out of his mouth.

Under the porch, the dog moved further back into the shadows. He didn't want any part of what was going on.

"Howdy, boys," Vincent said when he'd gotten the dust out. "What can we do for you."

"What're you doin' here, Sheriff?" Turley Ross asked, assuming what he considered to be his rightful role as spokesman. "You're supposed to be back in town, keepin' the citizens safe."

"My deputy's doin' that," Vincent said. He could feel his stomach churning. "You got a problem with that?"

"Not so long as you don't get in our way," Ross said. "You know what we're here for, all right."

"I guess maybe I do," Vincent said, looking over the crowd. "I'm kinda surprised to see you and your boys here, though, Mr. Benteen. You, too, Preacher."

"Just seeing justice done," Benteen said. He felt he had to say something.

Randall said nothing, just stared.

"Well, you won't be seein' much justice around here," Vincent said. "Paco ain't on the place. I've already searched." He reckoned he was on safe ground, since he was telling only half a lie. "The boy's gone off on his mule, the way I figger it. It's not to be found anywhere on the place."

"I don't believe that for a minute," Ross said, looking around him. "You boys know what kinda shape that kid was in. You believe he rode away from here on some mule?"

"Hell, no," Len Hawkins said. "I don't believe he could stand up, much less ride a mule."

"I don't know about that," Harl Case said. "If he wanted to get away bad enough, maybe he did ride off on that mule. Maybe we just oughta go on back to town and let the sheriff handle this business. He's the one who knows how."

Ross turned in his saddle and glared at Case. "Goddamn you, Harl, you yellow bastard. If you wanta go home, you go. But you don't try to speak for the rest of us. The sheriff's already let that kid out of jail once. We're gonna make sure he don't get out again."

"Damn right," Lane Harper said. "We want that boy, Sheriff, and we're gonna get him. Ain't that right, fellas?"

The cowboys yelled in agreement.

Vincent carefully kept his hand away from his gun. He could see they were all worked up, all except for Benteen and Case, who looked a little doubtful about the whole thing. And maybe excepting the preacher, too. The rest of them weren't quite at the point where they'd shoot their sheriff, but they weren't that far from it, either. He didn't know what to do except to keep on standing there and hoping they'd get tired of jawing and leave.

Vincent decided to try an appeal to Randall. "Preacher, you know this ain't right. The Bible teaches forgiveness, not takin' the law into your own hands. Vengeance is the Lord's, ain't that what it says?"

The sheriff had appealed to the wrong man. In his addled state, Randall did not recall any scriptures that encouraged forgiveness.

He looked at Vincent with his dead eyes and began to speak. His voice was quiet at first, but it rose in volume and power as he went along. "'And the Lord said to Moses, "If men strive, and hurt a woman with child, so that her fruit depart from her, and if any mischief follow, thou shalt give life for life"'!"

"Amen!" Ross Turley yelled.

"Eye for eye!" Randall said.

"Amen!" Turley yelled again, and this time Harper and Hawkins joined in.

"Tooth for tooth!"

"Amen!" They were all yelling now, except for Charley Davis, Harl Case, and Benteen.

"Hand for hand!"

"Amen!" Davis was with them by now.

"Foot for foot!"

"Amen! Amen!"

"Burning for burning!"

"Amen, Preacher, amen!"

"Wound for wound!"

"Amen, amen, amen!"

"Stripe for stripe!"

"You said it, Preacher! Amen! Amen!"

Randall fell silent, sitting rigid and staring straight ahead, but the other men were practically dancing in their saddles, laughing, talking, reaching out and slapping one another on the shoulder, yelling "Amen!" over and over. Vincent hadn't seen or heard anything like it in his whole life. He was sure sorry he had said anything to the preacher about forgiveness and revenge.

When they had calmed down some, Turley Ross said, "I guess that just about says it all, don't it, Sheriff? You gonna try and stop us now?"

Vincent felt like he might puke. "I ain't gonna stop you. I'm just sayin' that Paco ain't here." He wondered where Mrs. Morales was, what she and the little girls must be thinking.

"I'm sayin' he is here," Ross said. "I'm saying we're gonna find him."

"Wait a minute, Turley," Harl Case said. "Why would the sheriff lie to us? If the boy's gone, we'd just be wastin' our time here."

"I thought you'd gone home to suck your sugar tit, Harl," Ross said. There was laughter from the cowboys and from Harl's friends.

"He's got a point, though, Turley," Len Hawkins said. "What if the kid really did ride outa here on that mule? He's just gettin' that much further ahead of us while we mess around."

Turley thought about it for a minute. "Okay. You may be right. Maybe we oughta split up. Some of us can search the place here, and the rest go lookin' for the mule. We got any trackers in this bunch?"

The big cowboy called Frank spoke up. "I ain't no Injun, but I can read sign some. Anybody can show me where that mule started from, I can make a show to follow it."

"Yeah," Hawkins said. "If we can't find where the mule started from, maybe it didn't start at all."

That idea distracted them for a minute, but they soon found what most of them agreed to be fresh tracks around a little corral built of mesquite sticks not too far from the house.

Vincent didn't help them. He stood on the porch and watched.

Turley thought maybe it would be best if Harper and Hawkins went with Frank and the cowboys. "That way you can spread out some more if he's really out there and if he's smart enough to try layin' a false trail."

Everyone agreed that seemed like a good idea, and the men rode off, whooping and hollering. That left Randall, Moran, Benteen, Davis, Ross, and Case to search the property.

"Not very damn much to search," Ross pointed out. "Just the house, that shed over there, anyplace in the bushes where he might be hidin'."

"I'm tellin' you, he's not here," Vincent said from the porch.

"Yeah, you said that," Ross told him. "But we're gonna look just the same."

"Not me," Harl said. "I've had enough of this, Turley."

"Well, that's just fine with me, Harl. Why don't you go on home and knit yourself a shawl."

Harley's face burned, but he didn't say anything. He also made no move to leave.

"I'll do no searching, either," Benteen said. "I'm only here to see that things are done right."

Vincent thought that was a damn weak excuse, and he wondered if the man believed it.

"That's all right, Mr. Benteen," Ross said. "We've got enough fellas here to do the job."

Not counting Randall, Vincent thought. Randall didn't look up to doing anything beyond what he was doing, sitting there like some kind of statue.

"Davis, why don't you ride around, see what you can scare up in the scrub," Ross said. "Moran, you look in that shed. I'll look in the house myself."

Vincent knew that this was it. The direct challenge. He would either have to back down and let Ross in the house, or draw on him.

Then he thought of something that might delay the confrontation, if not prevent it entirely.

"Mr. Benteen," he said. "Did you know the Randall girl was pregnant when she died?"

"What?" Benteen said, startled. He braced his hands on his saddle horn and leaned forward.

"You heard what the preacher said, didn't you? About hurtin' a woman with child? He wasn't just talkin' the Bible there. He was talkin' about his daughter."

"Maybe so," Benteen said. "But what does that have to do with me?"

"I thought maybe you knew about Liz and Charley."

"I think you better shut up now, Sheriff,"

Charley said. "Mr. Benteen knows I ain't seen Liz for quite a spell."

"That ain't what you told me, Charley," Vincent said.

"What is this?" Ross said. "What's that have to do with anything?"

"Plenty," Vincent said. "Charley's probably the one that got her pregnant."

"What?" Benteen said. "What are you —"

"Goddamn you, Sheriff!" Charley said, his hand going for his gun.

Charley was fast, a lot faster than Vincent, who never thought of Charley drawing on him in the first place.

But Charley was not as fast as Kid Reynolds.

The preacher was confused in his mind. He almost felt he was three people in one — a preacher whose daughter had outraged him, a man seeking revenge for the death of a loved one, and Kid Reynolds, who was going to get that revenge.

Despite the fact that he hadn't handled a gun in so many years, neither Charley nor Vincent had cleared leather before Randall drew with a speed and skill that would have been the envy of many a man who practiced every day.

Randall's pistol boomed twice, and two shots hit Charley squarely in the chest.

Charley was gripping the reins with his left hand when the bullets hit him. His hand clenched, pulling backward. The horse reared and turned in a tight circle, reacting to the sudden tugging pressure on the bridle in its mouth. Then it pitched once and the reins slipped out of Charley's suddenly limp fingers as he slid off the saddle to the hard ground, landing on his back, the dark blood staining the front of his shirt.

The horse plunged off across the yard.

Vincent had his pistol out by then, but Randall had holstered his own weapon. He edged his horse over to Charley and looked down at him.

"'Rejoice, O ye nations, with his people: for he will avenge the blood of his servants, and will render vengeance to his adversaries.'"

Charley lay full length in the dust, his right leg twitching. He was trying to reach his pistol, but he couldn't move his arms. The dog came running from beneath the porch and stood over Charley, barking in his face.

"Son of a bitch," Charley said. "Son of a bitch."

Chapter Twenty-Seven

Benteen and Ross got Charley up on the porch out of the sun while the preacher sat on his horse and watched.

Vincent went inside for Mrs. Morales, to see if she had anything to dress Charley's wounds with, not that he thought it would do much good. Charley was lung-shot, you could tell. You could almost hear the air whistling in and out of the wound.

Moran wasn't much help. He didn't give a damn about Charley, and he was pretty much disgusted by the whole affair. He thought he'd ride around a little, look over the property, see if he could locate the kid. Moran figured that nobody would miss him. They were all too busy looking after the dying ranch foreman.

"Goddamn it, Charley," Benteen said. "Why didn't you tell me?"

"Don't know," Charley said. It was obviously an effort for him to speak. "I didn't kill that girl, though."

"Course you didn't kill her," Ross said. "We know who killed her. This is all the sheriff's fault."

"It's our fault," Harl said. He had put the shotgun down. "We shouldn't've come here. It was the wrong thing to do."

Consuela Morales came out of the house with some water and clean rags. She helped Vincent take off Charley's shirt, and then she bathed the wounds. They looked worse than Vincent had first thought.

"How's it look?" Charley said. He kept his eyes averted, looking at Benteen and Vincent.

"It ain't good," Benteen said.

"No use lyin'," Vincent said. "You prob'ly ain't gonna make it, Charley."

"Figgered. Hurts like hell. Wish you'd kept your damn mouth shut, Sheriff."

"Yeah," Vincent said. "Me, too. I shoulda known that preacher was crazy."

"Hell," Charley groaned. "I never saw a man as fast as that. And him a preacher."

"You messed with his daughter," Benteen said. "If you'd messed with mine, I'd've killed you, too." He was struck with a sudden thought. "Goddamn. *Did* you mess with my daughter, you son of a bitch?"

Charley coughed and bright red blood flowed over his chin. Consuela wiped it away.

She was sorry for the man, but he should not have come here looking for her son. The livery stable man, *Señor* Case, was right about that. Now that they had come, one man was already dying; there might be more before the day was over.

"I didn't mess with Lucille, not ever," Charley said when she had wiped the blood away. "I didn't mean for Liz to get pregnant, either. She went to the doc, but there wasn't anything he could do."

He coughed again, and again the blood came out. Consuela wiped it away.

"You didn't kill her, though," Ross said. "You said you didn't kill her."

"No. Hell, no. I didn't kill nobody."

"A dyin' man don't lie," Ross said. He stood up and went into the house. Vincent didn't try to stop him.

Charley coughed one more time. He died just as Willie, Jack, and Lucille rode into the yard.

Lucille didn't cry.

She didn't know why, but she just couldn't, not after she heard about Liz being pregnant. How could Charley have done that and not said anything? she wondered. To look at him lying there, you'd think he was as innocent as a baby, with those clear blue

244

eyes. Later she'd cry.

"We'd better go on home," Benteen told his daughter. His plans for her were ruined, and he no longer saw the need for finding the Morales boy. "There's been enough dying here already. I'll send Rankin for Charley when we get back to town."

"We can't go yet," Lucille said. "Mr. Turner has something to say."

"That's right, Sheriff," Jack said. "I wouldn't't've come out here otherwise."

"Don't worry about that, Jack," Vincent said. "What's this about Willie?"

"He says the Morales boy didn't kill Liz Randall," Lucille said. "He was there."

"Is that the truth, Willie?" Vincent said.

"Who the hell cares what a drunk says?" Ross said, emerging from his fruitless search of the house. "He wouldn't know the truth if it spit in his face."

"I know some things, all right," Willie said. "I can't remember everything, but I can remember some things."

"What do you know about Liz Randall?" Vincent said.

"I know that boy didn't kill her," Willie said, trying to sound as if he believed himself.

"How the hell do you know that?" Ross demanded.

"I was there," Willie said.

"You sayin' that *you* killed her?" Ross asked.

"No, I ain't sayin' that. I'm sayin' I was there. I saw her body, and then the Meskin kid came along. I hid from him, but then he heard me in the bushes and ran off. He didn't do anything."

"You ain't nothin' but a damn drunk," Ross said. "You don't know what you saw or when you saw it. I think you're lyin'."

"He's not lying," Lucille said. "Why would he lie?"

That stopped Ross for a minute, and Vincent said, "You didn't see who killed her?"

"I can't remember that part," Willie said.

"See what I'm tellin' you?" Ross said, his confidence restored. "You can't believe a word he says. He don't know what he saw and what he didn't see. I still think it was the kid."

"You can't be pos'tive, though," Harl said.

"We saw the kid, caught him in the act. He was there. He done it." That settled it as far as Ross was concerned.

Then he turned to Vincent. "And because you got things stirred up here, you've gone and got Charley Davis killed. It's as much your fault as anybody's. If you'd let us be, the preacher wouldn't've shot him."

"If you hadn't brought 'em out here, Charley would still be alive," Vincent said. "Maybe it's your fault as much as it is anybody's."

246

"I don't know who you think'd believe a thing like that," Ross said. "Now you do what you want to with Charley and the preacher. I'm gonna help Moran find that kid."

Paco was asleep when the shots were fired.

He didn't know how it had happened, but somehow he had drifted off. He was sweating heavily, and he had been dreaming of being in a burning building. It was a barn of some kind, with a high, beamed ceiling and a loft from which burning bales of hay were falling all around him, flying apart into flaming balls as he ran down a seemingly endless corridor of stalls filled with screaming horses that reared and kicked at the stall doors. The dream was so real that he could almost smell the smoke and hear the frantic neighing of the panicked horses.

The shots caused him to jerk awake, his hands clenching on the rifle, and he was momentarily disoriented. It was as if he were still in the burning barn, and he fought to get to his feet to flee the flames that were licking out at him, the bales that were falling like blazing comets.

The pain in his arm and side let him know that he was not going to get up very fast, and then he came to himself. He remembered that he was in the tiny shed, that he was hiding

247

from men who wanted to kill him, and that he had to be alert to everything that happened.

He got his eye to one of the cracks in the wall, and he could see there were people in the yard, men on horses, and that some of them were looking at another man who was on the ground. Paco didn't know for sure what had happened, but it seemed that the man had been shot.

Why he had been shot was not all clear, until Paco saw that one of the men was the preacher. These men had come for Paco, but they had killed someone else.

Paco watched as the wounded man was carried to the porch. He saw that the preacher did not dismount to help, nor did one of the other men, someone whom Paco did not recognize.

That man, when the others were occupied with the wounded one, left the preacher and began to ride his horse slowly around the yard. Paco soon lost sight of him.

Other riders came into the yard. One of them was Jack Simkins, whose face was easily recognizable, and one of them was Willie Turner. Paco did not know the woman.

There was some sort of argument on the porch. Paco wondered what it was about. Maybe they were arguing about him, about where he was. He had to be ready for them.

If they came for him, he would not hesitate. His finger found the trigger of the rifle, and its pressure comforted him.

Lane Harper heard the shots and pulled up on the reins. His horse came to a stop, and Harper listened to see if there would be any more shooting.

He had gotten behind the other riders when he had stopped to go off down a side trail that led into a dry wash, but he hadn't found anything. When he rode out again, the others had gone on ahead and turned a bend that led them around a sizable hill; they probably hadn't heard anything.

When no more shots came, Harper wondered if his ears were playing tricks on him. If they'd found the Morales kid, there'd've been more shots than two, wouldn't there?

Harper smoothed his mustache with the thumb and first finger of his right hand, wiping the sweat on his shirt when he was done. He hoped they would find the kid soon and do what they had to do.

He wondered for the first time why he was so eager to do it. The kid had never done anything to him. Was it because of the first killing and the fact that Harper had played a part in covering for the gambler?

Or was it because they had beat the kid so

damn bad last night and wanted to prove they had a right to do it?

Harper didn't know, but when he thought about it, both reasons seemed pretty damn weak to him. He wondered if he was getting yellow, like Harl Case or Mr. Danton.

Not that he would ever have called Mr. Danton yellow to his face, but Lane thought that was what the man was, all right. He had got so that he was scared even to come to his own place of business, all because of the shooting that had occurred there. He had just about turned the whole thing over to Lane, and now all Mr. Danton wanted to do was sit in his little house with the shades drawn and get drunk. The few times he'd come back to the saloon, Lane could smell the liquor on him, though he was the very one who'd told Lane that the one thing a saloonkeeper couldn't afford to do was to drink.

It was advice Lane had taken to heart, even more so after seeing Danton the last few times he'd come into the saloon. Lane drank, but never more than a couple of shots a day.

Lane couldn't figure Mr. Danton. The man was a good boss; he paid on time, and kept his nose out of the bar business and let Lane run it the way it ought to be run. He had his pick of all the girls who worked the saloon. But the shooting had taken it out of him. He was more like a ghost now than a man. Come to think of it, Lane hadn't seen him in the daytime for more than a year. He came to the saloon only after dark, after most of the citizens were off the street. Lane wondered briefly if Mr. Danton had ever run into Liz Randall on his moonlight walks to the saloon, but he dismissed the thought.

Lane knew nothing would ever get to him like the shooting of Morales had gotten to Danton, so why was he worrying about the damn kid?

Then he thought of a reason he might be worried. What if the kid hadn't done anything, and whoever killed that Randall girl was still on the loose? That might make a difference. It might mean that someone else could get killed.

He put that thought out of his mind. If people couldn't watch out for themselves, that wasn't Lane Harper's fault. He was going to take care of the fella who really mattered — himself — and to hell with the rest of 'em.

That was why they had to get the Morales kid, he guessed. They had to show that they were right and that they were taking care of themselves in the way they were supposed to, and taking care of the rest of the town, too.

But what if there was another killing and they were proved wrong?

251

Harper took off his hat and wiped his shirtsleeve across his forehead.

We weren't wrong, he told himself. We done the right thing. And if we didn't, no one would know it when the kid was dead. That was a good enough reason to find him and get him out of the way once and for all.

He clucked to his horse, getting her into a trot. He needed to catch up with the others.

He had already forgotten hearing the shots.

Chapter Twenty-Eight

Harper caught up with them just as they found the mule.

It was grazing on some dead grass that stuck up from between the rocks at the bottom of a narrow gully.

"How you reckon he got down there?" Frank asked no one in particular. He was slightly embarrassed that he had lost the mule's trail. They had only found the cussed thing by accident.

"Hell," one of the cowhands said, "you never know about a mule. I wouldn't be surprised if it flew."

There was a hackamore on the mule's head. A rope was attached to the hackamore.

"You reckon the kid was ridin' it?" Len Hawkins asked. "I sure as to God don't see him anywhere."

"He coulda fell off," a cowboy ventured. "Might be lyin' somewhere in that ditch."

"I bet he ain't," someone else said. "I don't

think anybody could ride with a riggin' like that."

"You can't never tell about a Meskin," another said. "They might ride like that, for all you know."

"More likely that sorry beast was tied up somewheres with that rope and just pulled loose."

Len Hawkins thought that was probably true. "That means the kid's back at the house and they set this mule to lead us off. Good thing we didn't all come after it, or the kid'd be hid somewhere else by now and we might never find him."

"I still think we better check things out around here," Frank said. "Just in case he fell off. You said he was beat up pretty bad."

"Yeah, he was," Hawkins said. "What do you think, Lane?"

Harper thought that the kid was back at the house, just like Len did, but he didn't want to take a chance on missing him if he wasn't.

"We better look," he said.

The men got off their horses and went down into the gully, sliding on the dirt and the small stones that formed its sides. The mule didn't pay much attention to them. It just kept on eating, grabbing the tufts of dry grass in its thick yellow teeth and pulling them into its mouth.

"Damn," one of the cowboys said. "Wouldn't nothin' in the world but a mule eat that stuff. It ain't nothin' but spear grass and burrs."

"That's why you oughta be on a mule if you're gonna take a trip through a desert," Frank said. "You can count on the mule gettin' through it. Course, you might not."

The men walked in both directions, but there was no sign of Paco in the gully. It widened out finally and there were places where a mule could easily have walked down into it, but there was no way to tell if the mule had been there. The ground was just too hard.

"We better go on back," Lane said. He suddenly remembered the two shots that he had heard. "That kid ain't nowhere around here."

"Not unless he fell off the mule on the way to this gully," Frank said. "As beat up as you say he was, he mighta died on the way."

"If he did, the buzzards'll find him before we do," Hawkins said. "Let's go back."

They were climbing out of the gully when someone asked what to do about the mule.

"Leave the damn thing here," Hawkins said. "It'll get home by itself, and if it don't, it can starve."

"Not much danger of that, long as there's some of that dead stuff around to chaw on," Frank said. "It'll be okay."

They mounted up and left the mule, which watched them incuriously as they rode away. Then it dipped its head and began to pull patiently at the grass.

Moran gave an occasional look at the porch as he walked his horse around the property, but he wasn't too interested in the fate of the cowboy. Moran was pretty sure the fella was going to die. Not many people survived two shots in the chest like that.

Kinda funny that the preacher was the one to kill somebody, though, Moran thought. And even funnier that the preacher could use a gun like that. It was out and fired and back in the holster before you could hardly blink your eye. Where'd a preacher learn to shoot like that, anyhow?

He steered the horse around the little corral. Nothing there to look at.

He saw Ross leave the porch and go inside the house. Hell, he should know the kid wouldn't be in there. The sheriff didn't have any reason to lie about that.

There was a sort of chicken house, not much more than a lean-to, really, in back of the house. Moran rode over to it. He could no longer see what was going on in front, but he didn't care.

There was a bit of shade in the chicken

house, but that was about all. A couple of nests, too, and one of 'em looked like it had an egg in it.

A roost made of a couple of sticks with cross-pieces nailed on was leaning against the chicken house. The roost was thick with dried chicken droppings and the ground beneath it was covered with them. The smell bothered Moran, and he turned the horse away to inspect the skimpy bushes that grew around the edges of the property.

As he rode back around the house, he could see that several other people had arrived there. He wondered vaguely who they were, but he was sure they were of no consequence to him.

The boy wasn't in any of the bushes, and Moran hadn't expected him to be. There was just one other place to look, and Moran had been saving that. There was a little shed, hardly big enough for anybody to be hiding in, that the gambler was going to check last. If there really was anyone hiding on the place, the shed was where they'd be.

He rode over there.

The door was latched on the outside, but that didn't mean anything. Moran got off his horse and pulled his .44. He wanted to have it ready just in case. He cocked the hammer.

He pulled the stick out of the hasp, flipped

the hasp back, and opened the door, his pistol ready.

Paco Morales shot him in the face.

Lane Harper heard the shot. "Goddamn, they're shootin' again!"

"Again?" Len Hawkins said. "What the hell do you mean by that?"

"I forgot to tell you. I thought I heard some shootin' awhile back, when I was behind you."

"That's a hell of a thing to forget," Frank said. "Let's get on back there fast."

The cowboys put the spurs to their horses, drawing their guns and whooping as they rode. Len and Harper trailed behind, holding on to their shotguns as best they could, eating dust.

Paco saw the man coming through the glare of the sun. He pulled his eye away from the hole and got ready. His mother had told him to hide, but he was not going to hide. He was not going to let them just come in the shed and find him there trying to cover himself like a coward. He was ashamed that he had gone so far as to get inside the shed. He should have stayed outside and confronted the men from the beginning.

He did not know the man who was getting off the horse, but that did not matter to him. If the man opened the door, he was an enemy.

Paco was going to treat him as such.

The thought of killing the man did not frighten Paco. He believed that the man would certainly kill, or at least take him back to the jail to await hanging. Paco was not going back, even if he had to kill to prevent it.

Then the man got off the horse, and when he drew his gun, Paco was even more certain of what he had to do. This was not the time to think about a fair fight. His life was on the line, and he was not going to give the man a chance.

Paco heard the stick being taken from the hasp. His finger tightened on the trigger.

The door swung open. Paco pulled the trigger.

Vincent was watching when it happened, as was Consuela Morales. There was something in her eyes that told the sheriff that her son was in that shed, and he almost called out a warning, whether to the boy or to Moran, he wasn't sure. He hesitated for just a second, and then it was too late.

There was the booming of a rifle and the back of the gambler's head flew off.

Moran's hands went up in the air, and his pistol went flying up as the gambler took three steps backward, his whole body wobbling like he was trying to keep his balance. You could tell he wasn't going to be able to do it, though.

Sure enough, he fell, but he didn't fall backward. He tilted that way; then he tilted forward and fell on his face, what was left of it.

His pistol hit a little before he did, discharging a single shot into the air.

Turley Ross whirled around and jumped off the porch, running toward the shed by the time the echo of the shot had died, drawing his pistol as he ran.

Vincent hesitated for a moment and then went after him, knowing pretty much what had happened. He didn't want to get involved in it, but it was too late to worry about that. He was going to have to stop Ross before something worse happened.

The preacher twitched the reins of his horse, turning its head toward town. Without a backward glance, he rode out of the yard, no longer interested in the proceedings. His job was done.

Harl Case sat on the edge of the porch, shaking his head. He put down the shotgun. He knew that he wasn't going to use it. Not now. Not ever.

Benteen did not know what to do. He put his arm protectively around his daughter, while Willie Turner looked around for a place to hide.

Consuela Morales stood there on the porch, crying silently, tears running down her cheeks.

Vincent caught up with Ross halfway to the shed and jumped for him, grabbing him around his broad shoulders and bearing him to the ground.

Ross got to his feet and shook Vincent off like a dog shaking off water. Vincent fell on his back, losing his breath. He hadn't realized Ross was so strong.

By now, Jack was on his way to help. Ross heard him pounding across the dirt and pulled his gun.

Vincent heard the hammer cock. He was still gasping for breath and couldn't get up, but he knew he had to do something. He tried kicking at Ross's ankle just as Ross pulled the trigger.

He connected weakly, but it was enough to throw Ross's aim off. The bullet intended for Jack plowed up the earth in front of him instead.

Jack got his own gun out, but he couldn't shoot on the run; the risk of hitting Vincent was too great.

Ross turned and fired two shots at the shed. He missed the door, but both bullets cracked through the wooden sides of the building.

Vincent thought that he heard a cry from inside, but he wasn't sure. He got to his knees and drew his gun.

He might have gotten off a shot, but just then

the riders came thundering back down the trail. Vincent didn't want to hit any of them.

For that matter, he didn't want to hit Turley Ross. He didn't want to shoot anyone at all. He wanted to be sitting back in his hot little jail, thinking about what he'd be eating for lunch. He was right in the middle of what he'd spent years trying to avoid, and it was even worse than he'd thought it would be.

Ross was running toward the riders, yelling at the top of his voice.

"He's in the shed! He's in the goddamn shed!"

The men were reining in, trying to stop from running Ross down. The horses were shying away from the body and the smell of blood.

As soon as they got their horses stopped, the men had their guns out. Harper was trying to cock the sawed-off, and Len Hawkins was working on the Winchester.

"He's killed the goddamn gambler!" one of the cowboys yelled. "Let's get the little bastard."

Jack ran past Vincent, who was headed for the shed. By the time Vincent got there, Jack was already standing in front of the open door.

"You in there Paco?" Vincent said.

"I am here," Paco answered weakly. "I have been shot."

"Damn," Jack said. "They beat the hell out of him, and now he's shot."

"I thought you didn't have much of a taste for this kinda thing anymore, Jack," Vincent said.

"I didn't think so, either," Jack answered. "But I think the kid oughta get a fair shake. So far, we ain't done too much for him."

Consuela Morales was wailing something from the porch, but Vincent couldn't understand her. Lucille Benteen was standing with her over the body of Charley, trying to comfort her.

Benteen and Willie Turner were walking slowly across the yard.

It might have been Consuela's wails that attracted Harper's eye to the porch. "Jesus. Did he kill Charley, too?"

"Naw, the preacher did that," Ross said. "But that don't matter. That kid's right here. We gotta take care of him."

"Why did the preacher kill Charley?" Frank said. "What the hell did Charley do to the preacher?"

Ross shook his head in disgust. "I said that don't matter. What matters is that we got the kid right here in that shed."

The interior of the shed was dark, and Vincent and Simkins were standing in front of the door. No one could see exactly what was inside, if anything.

"That right, Sheriff?" Len Hawkins said. "Is that kid in there?"

"He's in here," Vincent said, trying to hide the nervousness in his voice. "I'll be takin' him back to town. You boys just ride on off now."

"We ain't goin' nowhere without that kid," Ross said. "Get outa the way, Sheriff. You, too, Jack."

Vincent kept his voice as steady as he could. "We're not moving, Turley. We're the law, remember?"

"Bullshit," Ross answered. "You let that boy get away once, and you'd do it again. We don't aim for it to happen that way. We're gonna see that he gets what's comin' to him and gets it right now. That right, fellas?"

The cowboys cheered him. A couple of them fired their pistols in the air.

"See what I'm tellin' you, Sheriff?" Ross said. "We're the law now. There's a time for talkin' and there's a time for hangin'. This here's a time for hangin'. Who's got a rope?"

Three or four of the cowboys pulled their lariats loose from the saddle ties and slapped them against their legs or waved them overhead.

"Here we go, Turley!"

"Use mine, fellas. It ain't even broke in yet!"

"This'un here's just made for neck stretch-in'!"

Vincent looked at Jack. He didn't know what to say to his deputy, but Jack didn't seem to need any encouragement. His face was set and determined.

I guess it's my job to be standing here, Vincent thought. He wondered if they'd kill him or just beat him, the way they'd beaten Paco. Either way, there were too many of 'em. He knew he didn't stand a chance, but the thought of leaving never entered his head. He didn't want to be there, but he was the sheriff.

One way or the other, he was in for the finish.

It didn't have to be that way for Jack, however.

"You better go on back over to the house, Jack." he said.

Jack smiled crookedly, his scarred face twisting. "Naw, I think I'll stay here. If I'd just let 'em kill him last night, we wouldn't be in this mess."

Vincent grinned back at him. "That's one way to look at it, I guess. You think you're worth all this trouble, Paco?"

There was no answer from inside the shed.

Chapter Twenty-Nine

Paco tried to answer, but he could not. His mouth had gone suddenly dry, and the dream of the fire was returning, seeping into his head against his will, though he tried to remain awake. He knew that he was bleeding from the bullet wound, but there was so much pain in his body that he could not even tell where he had been hit.

He could hear the horses screaming and kicking at the stalls that trapped them.

The bales of fire began to fall, and Paco began to flee down the endless corridors of the barn.

"Reckon he's dead?" Jack said.

"I don't know," Vincent said, thinking that it would be a hell of a note if he and Jack were to die defending a kid who was already past saving. It made about as much sense as anything else that had happened, he guessed.

"Why don't you get that gambler out of the

sun," he told Jack. The deputy put his gun away and grabbed the dead man under the arms, trying to avoid the bloody remains of his head. Then he dragged him over to the side of the shed while Vincent stood in front of the door.

Moran's boots dragged little trails on the dirt, and Jack laid him down in the shade. Then he came back to stand with the sheriff.

By that time, Benteen and Willie had arrived to join them at the door.

Willie plainly didn't want to be there. His eyes were darting to the left and right, looking for a way to escape, but Benteen had a firm grip on his upper arm and there was no way he could get free. The sight of Moran's body clearly wasn't making him feel any better.

"This ain't your fight, Benteen," Vincent said. "Charley and that damn gambler are already dead. No use in you and Willie windin' up the same way."

"We won't," Benteen said. "Willie here has something he wants to say."

Benteen was sorry he had ever come to the Morales place. He knew now that he had been wrong, that he had been stupid to believe that getting the Morales boy out of the way would make things all right for Charley and Lucille. Charley was dead, and maybe he deserved to be, but Benteen did not have to contribute any more to the stupidity and the violence that Liz Randall's death had begun. Hearing Willie's story had convinced him that he had to extricate himself from a situation that he had found disagreeable in the first place. Now he had been given a chance to stop the rock from rolling down the hill, and he was going to take it.

"We don't have to listen to some drunk spout off about his delirious trembles," Ross said. "You get out of the way, Mr. Benteen, and take that drunk with you."

"Wait a minute, Ross," Vincent said. "Why don't you let these men hear for themselves what Willie has to say? It might surprise 'em."

"You saw what talkin' did for Charley," Ross said. "He prob'ly ain't too happy about lettin' you spout off to that preacher."

Vincent got the point, but he still thought he had to let the men hear Willie. Maybe they would believe him.

"You don't speak for me or my men, Mr. Ross," Benteen said, determined that Willie was going to be heard. "They're going to listen to Willie if I say so. Isn't that right, men?"

The cowboys who had pulled their lariats were already tying them back to the saddles.

"We'll listen if you think we ought to, Mr. Benteen," Frank said. "You're the boss man."

Ross knew when he was whipped. "All right.

We'll listen. But I don't know who you think'll believe a drunk."

"We'll see," Benteen said. "Tell them, Willie."

Willie had never needed a drink more in his life, not even on the day his wife died. He swallowed once, and it felt like his Adam's apple was going to stick in his throat. He swallowed again, and it wasn't much better.

"Hell, I don't even believe he can talk," Ross said. "Why don't you just get outa the way, Willie, and let us go about our business."

"Yeah, Willie," Len Hawkins said. "Why don't you just do that."

"Don't let 'em bother you, Willie," Vincent said. "Go on and say your piece."

Willie tried again. This time he got it out. "I don't think the kid — Paco — I don't think he's the one that killed the preacher's girl."

"There it is, then," Ross said. "That about does it, sure enough. The biggest drunk in Dry Springs don't think the kid did it. I guess all you fellas are satisfied now, ain't you?"

He laughed, and most of the others joined in.

"Tell 'em why you think the way you do, Willie," Vincent said.

Willie swallowed again. "I . . . I was there."

The laughter stopped short. Some of the men stirred uneasily in their saddles.

"You was there," Ross snarled. "You was there. Well, if you was there, tell us who did kill her, then." Ross already knew that Willie couldn't answer that one.

"I don't know," Willie said. He looked down at the ground.

"See there?" Ross said. "He ain't got no more idea than a rabbit about who killed that girl. Get outa the way, Willie, and you won't get hurt."

Willie would have moved then, but Benteen still had hold of his arm. Benteen may have looked soft, but he had a grip like a bear's claw.

"Tell them the rest of it, Willie," Benteen said.

"I . . . I was there when the kid came by," Willie said. "She was dead when he got there."

"That's a damn lie!" Ross yelled. "We caught him in the act! We was there, too!"

"No, you weren't," Willie said, adding something that Ross had not heard earlier. He said it so soft that Vincent thought nobody would hear him, but they did.

"What?" Len Hawkins said. "You callin' us liars, you drunk son of a bitch?"

"I ain't callin' you anything," Willie said. "I'm just sayin' you weren't there when the kid come along, and I was. That's all."

"I oughta kill you right now," Ross said.

"I don't think so," Benteen said. "Not right now."

"You tellin' me that you believe this damn drunk, Mr. Benteen?" Ross said. "Jesus, he's just —"

"I know what he is," Benteen said. "But I think he saw something last night, something that casts a doubt on the boy's guilt. I'm taking my men home."

He looked at Vincent. "I'm not saying the boy's innocent, but I'm not going to have anything to do with hanging him. You're on your own now, Sheriff."

He turned back to his men. "We're pulling out of here. You can come, too, Willie."

Still holding Willie by the arm, he started back to the house, not even looking back to see if his men were following.

The cowboys were looking at one another and at the retreating back of the man who paid their wages.

"What do you think, Frank?" one of them said finally.

"Hell, I think we better follow the boss," Frank said, nudging his mount gently. "Let's go."

The others moved aside for him.

"You don't mean you're gonna take the word of a yella drunk?" Ross said. "A man that ain't seen a sober day in no tellin' how many years?"

"I don't give a damn about him, tell you the truth," Frank said. "But I know where my money comes from." He kept on going, and the other ranch hands followed him.

When Benteen reached the porch, he stopped to wait for his daughter. She gave Mrs. Morales one last comforting hug and stepped off the porch to join her father. The cowboys waited a respectful distance behind.

When Lucille got on her horse, Harl Case got up from the porch and climbed on his own. He didn't look at the men by the shed.

Benteen and his daughter rode slowly out of the yard, followed by the cowboys. Harl Case and Willie trailed along behind.

"Goddamn that Harl," Ross muttered. He, Harper, and Len Hawkins were left to face the sheriff and his deputy.

Vincent liked the odds better than he had earlier, but he was still uneasy. Those two shotguns were enough to level him, Jack, and the shed besides. Without reloading.

He caught a movement out of the corner of his eye. Consuela Morales was walking across the yard. The sun glinted on the barrel of the shotgun she carried, the one Harl had left behind. She was carrying it purposefully, as if she knew how to use it. She was no longer crying. Her eyes were dry and hard.

The odds were getting better all the time, Vincent thought.

"It's over, fellas," Vincent said. "You might's well go on back to town. We got two dead men here, maybe one in the shed. No use havin' anymore."

Ross's face was flaming, and not because of the heat. He was irate about the way things had worked out. He had been for a short time the leader of a whole crowd, but now he was down to only two other men. The sheriff had no business being there, and then that damn Benteen girl had to turn up with Willie Turner. It could all have been so simple, but it just hadn't worked out the way it should.

Turley Ross wasn't going to turn tail, though. If the sheriff thought that, he was dead wrong. Ross was going to get the kid and he was going to see that the kid got what was coming to him.

"I ain't goin' nowhere, Sheriff," he said. "Neither are these other two. So why don't you just step aside and let me look in that shed. If the kid's dead, well, then maybe we'll go on back to town."

"If he's dead, I'll be takin' you to the jail," Vincent surprised himself by saying. "For murder," he added.

Ross took a deep breath, swelling his chest,

then let the air out slowly.

"You son of a bitch," he said. "You wouldn't dare to do that to me."

"Yes, he would," Jack said. "I'd help him, if he needed any help." Vincent was as surprised at Jack as he had been at himself, though he shouldn't have been. Jack had already showed he had nerve last night.

Consuela Morales walked behind them then, entering the shed and bending over her son.

"How's the boy?" Vincent asked.

"He is alive," Consuela said. "I think. But he is very sick. He is bleeding." She turned to stand in the doorway, the shotgun trained on Ross.

"Looks like we got a standoff here," Vincent said. "Why don't you fellas let us get this boy to the doc. I'll see that he stays in the jail this time and that he stands his trial. We'll let the law decide if he's guilty."

"He's guilty," Ross said. "Ain't that right, fellas?"

"Damn right, he is," Len Hawkins said.

Harper didn't say anything for a minute. He was beginning to wonder if this was worth it. Two men dead. The kid beat to hell, maybe shot.

But Harper had been there in the grove. He'd beat the kid along with the others.

"Yeah," he said. "He's guilty, all right."

"So," Ross said.

"Yeah," Vincent said. "Where does that leave us, though? You want to try killin' all of us? It seems likely you could do it, but one or two of you won't come out of it without a few holes in you."

Ross saw the logic of that. He didn't want to get killed, but at the same time he wanted to get the kid.

"Let's leave it," Harper said suddenly. "We can leave him to the law. If he's guilty, he'll swing. We don't have to be the ones to do it."

"If he's hurt pretty bad, he might not even make it to the trial," Hawkins said, not mentioning the fact that Vincent would consider Ross guilty of murder in that case. "Maybe we oughta give it up."

Vincent watched Ross's reaction. The stocky man ground his teeth; he was furious.

But he was not stupid. He could see that things were not in his favor any longer, if they had ever been. It was time for a decision.

"Goddammit," he said with clenched teeth.

"If you drop it now," Vincent said, "you better not try anything else. I've had about all I can stand of this." His voice was a little strained; he hoped it was convincing.

"All right," Ross said, his shoulders suddenly slumping. "To hell with it." He slipped his pistol in its holster and turned to walk away. Harper and Hawkins turned their horses to follow after him.

Vincent felt the tension drain out of him. Behind him, Consuela lowered the shotgun, and Jack heaved a slow sigh of relief.

Vincent was about to look in the shed when Ross whirled back, whipping out the pistol.

He got off a shot, flame spewing from the muzzle. The bullet passed right between Jack and Vincent and hit Consuela. The force of the bullet shoved her backward, and she fell on top of Paco. As she fell, she jerked the barrel of the single-shot Whitney up and pulled the trigger.

Harper and Hawkins, though taken by surprise as much as the others, were spinning in their saddles, trying to get their weapons in position to fire.

Vincent and Jack were dropping to the ground when the buckshot from Consuela's gun sizzled over their heads. The pattern was already spreading when the shot got to the two men on horseback, but it was still concentrated enough to shred Len Hawkins's left arm, throwing him hard to the right and out of the saddle.

Vincent was half lying on his pistol and scrabbling to get it out of the holster when

Jack started firing. The deputy wasn't hitting anybody, but he was keeping Harper too busy to fire the sawed-off.

Hawkins was lying on the ground now, screaming. No one was paying him any attention. They could hardly hear him, anyway; their ears were ringing from all the shooting.

Ross shot at the sheriff again, once or twice, but his aim was no better than Jack's. At least one of the bullets whacked into the dry wood of the shed. Vincent wasn't counting the shots, however, so he didn't know for sure how many times Ross had fired.

The sheriff finally got his pistol out. He shot twice at Ross, and the stocky man staggered back on his heels, dropping his pistol.

He bent to pick it up, but he couldn't seem to reach it. Looking at Vincent, he sat slowly down. A red stain was spreading on the front of his shirt.

Vincent felt sick. He hadn't really meant to hit him.

Ross kept his eyes on the sheriff as he felt around for his pistol. When his fingers closed on it, he cocked it and fired again, missing everyone, even missing the shed.

Harper broke open the sawed-off and pulled out the cartridges that he had never fired.

"I'm done," he said, laying the gun across

his lap and putting his hands in the air. "Give it up, Turley."

Hawkins stopped screaming. He lay on the ground, twisting and moaning. His horse had run away.

"I ain't givin' anything up," Ross said. He had made his play, and he was sticking with it. No one was going to say that Turley Ross turned yellow at the end. No one was going to laugh at him and call him a monkey again.

He was having trouble holding the pistol; it felt heavier than he thought it should, but somehow he kept it level.

He wondered if he had enough strength in his thumb to cock the hammer. He began pulling it back.

"Goddammit, Turley," Harper said.

Turley looked at him and smiled. "Ain't it the truth?" he said. Then he looked at Vincent. He got the hammer cocked.

"Lay the damn thing down, Turley," Vincent said.

"Can't do that, Sheriff. I got to finish it, show folks that I was right."

"This ain't right or wrong, Turley," Vincent said. "It's just downright stupid."

It looked to him like Ross was leaning over to one side. Maybe if he could keep him talking, he'd drop the gun.

"Turley, it ain't too late to call this off. You

put the gun down, and we'll —"

Turley pulled the trigger.

The bullet hit the shed, high up near the roof.

"Damn," Turley said. He thumbed back the hammer.

"Stop it, Turley," Harper said. "Dammit, just stop it now."

"Can't," Turley said. The hammer clicked into place.

Vincent shot him. The bullet hit Turley square in the chest, knocking him back and flipping him over. He looked like he was doing a backwards somersault. It would have been funny if Turley hadn't been dead.

Chapter Thirty

The Reverend Randall rode home, got off his horse, and went inside. His wife was there, sitting at the kitchen table. She looked up when her husband walked in.

She didn't look good to him. Her eyes were red from crying, and her fat face was even puffier than usual. For a minute he wondered who she was and what she was doing there.

For an even longer time, he wondered who *he* was.

"Where've you been?" she said when he didn't speak. "Don't you care that your daughter's over there in the funeral home? Don't you even want to see her one last time?"

It all came back to him then, who the woman was and why she was crying. He looked at her without pity. "'Let the dead bury their dead: but go thou and preach the kingdom of God.'"

She pushed her chair back and got to her feet. "You haven't preached the kingdom of God in years," she said. "I don't think you ever did. I don't know why I didn't see it before. God knows, and I should have known — the way you treated Liz, the way you treated me. You don't serve God, never have. You serve the devil."

Randall looked at her, but his eyes were not seeing her. In reality he was looking into himself, as deeply into himself as he could see.

What he saw there only he could say. Whether it was good or evil, whether it was Randall or Reynolds, he gave no sign. Perhaps it was neither, or both.

Or perhaps he saw nothing at all.

"What's the matter with you?" Martha said. "Can't you say anything? Isn't there anything in your head except those Bible verses?"

He kept on staring, seeing or not seeing.

"Quote the Bible, then. Go ahead. It won't change anything. It won't make you anything but what you are."

His mind clicked in again. "What I am," he said.

"That's right," she said. "I know what you are. God knows, too."

"God knows what I am," he said tonelessly.

He thought of his daughter, dead.

He thought of the man he had killed today, of the men he had killed years ago, of the lie that his life had been. Kid Reynolds was not his past. Kid Reynolds had never died. Kid

Reynolds had killed Randall's daughter as surely as he had killed her lover.

Kid Reynolds had killed Martha, too. Surely this woman, this grossly fat woman who stared and yelled at him, was not Martha.

Randall pulled the pistol once again. He looked at it as if it were a snake that might strike him.

"What are you doing?" Martha said. "Put that back!"

He looked at her stonily. "'If thy right eye offend thee, pluck it out and cast it from thee.'"

She looked fearfully at the gun. "What? What is that supposed to mean? Are you the one who cut my daughter?"

"No," he said, "I never touched her. I would never have hurt her willingly. She was my daughter, too." He looked at Martha for a second longer. Then he said, "'And if thy right hand offend thee, cut it off and cast it from thee.'"

Martha started crying again. "I don't understand," she said. "I don't understand."

Randall sighed, as if he were very tired. "Neither do I," he said wearily. "Neither do I."

He cocked the pistol, put it to his head, and pulled the trigger.

Vincent and Simkins got up and stood looking at Turley Ross for a minute.

"He wasn't a bad fella," Simkins said. "I guess he just went a little crazy."

"I guess we all did, but that don't make him any less dead," Harper said. "What about Len?"

"You can see about him," Vincent said. He turned to look in the shed to check on Mrs. Morales and Paco.

Mrs. Morales was conscious and trying to sit up. Vincent helped her. Ross's bullet had passed through her shoulder, and Vincent thought she would be all right after they got the bleeding stopped.

Paco did not look quite so good. He had been shot in the arm, the one that had not been broken in the beating. It looked to Vincent as if it might be broken now.

"We've got to get him to a doctor," Vincent told Jack. "His mother, too."

"Rankin oughta be here pretty soon," Jack said. "That is, if Benteen told him to come for Charley like he said he was."

"That's right," Vincent said. "We can use his wagon."

"He's gonna have quite a load," Jack said. "He'll have more bodies than he thought for."

"They can wait."

"Mighty hot," Jack said.

"They won't mind," Vincent told him.

"What about Len?" Harper called out. "He's hurt mighty bad. Looks like this arm might have to come off."

They heard Hawkins groan aloud at that remark.

"There'll be room in Rankin's wagon for him, too," Vincent said. "Unless you want to throw him across a saddle and let him get to town that way."

"He'd never make it," Harper said. "He's still bleedin' pretty bad."

"Then he'll just have to wait for the wagon," Vincent said. "See if you can do anything to help him, Jack."

While Jack was trying to get Len's bleeding stopped, Harper walked over to join Vincent. "I'm sorry about all this," he said. "We never meant for anybody to get killed."

"You meant for Paco to get killed," Vincent reminded him.

"Yeah," Harper admitted. "I guess we did. I guess we were wrong about that." He thought for a minute. "Who killed that gambler?" he asked.

"Paco," Vincent said. "But if you're thinking that makes him guilty of killin' the girl, you're wrong."

In fact, Vincent was now convinced that Paco was innocent of Liz Randall's murder.

Somewhere in among all the shooting and the scrambling, the things he'd been thinking about had come together in his mind. He was pretty sure he knew now who had killed the girl.

"I wasn't thinkin' he killed the girl," Harper said.

"It is a good thing you were not," Consuela Morales said, speaking for the first time. Her face was shiny with sweat. Though she must have been in pain, her voice was strong.

"What were you thinkin', then?" Vincent said.

"I don't know if I oughta say it."

"Say it."

"I guess I was just thinkin' that it was one of those things that was meant to happen," Harper said. "Sooner or later, I mean. That gambler killed the kid's daddy, you know."

"I was kinda surprised to see him show up here," Vincent admitted.

"He just rode into town today," Harper said. He hesitated, but it was plain he had more to say. He pulled off his hat and rubbed a hand across his slicked-down hair.

"Go on," Vincent said. "If you've got somethin' to say, spit it out."

Harper put the hat back on. "Hell, it probably don't matter. Turley's dead and Harl's turned tail. Len sure as hell won't care."

"Say it, then."

"The kid's daddy. He didn't pull any knife on that gambler. The gambler carried that knife in his boot and he put it in Morales's hand after he shot him. Morales called him a cheater, and the gambler shot him. We backed him up because he was a white man. That's the long and the short of it."

"Damn," Vincent said.

"Yeah," Harper agreed. "I don't think you oughta do anything to the kid for killin' that bastard. The kid was just doin' what was right."

"It wasn't right," Vincent said.

"It was justice," Mrs. Morales said. Her eyes were aglow with either pain or pride. "I knew that my husband was murdered and that my son was not a killer; he would not have shot that man if he had been left alone."

"You're probably right," Vincent said.

When they got back to town, Vincent waited while Doc Bigby, still relentlessly cheerful, saw to Consuela Morales and Paco first, over Hawkins's vehement objections.

"Goddammit, I'm a white man, Vincent!" he said. "You can't mean to get those two greasers taken care of before the doc gets a look at me!"

"I'd watch how I was talkin' if I were you,

Len," Vincent said. "Anybody that throws down on the sheriff with a shotgun is likely to be in a whole lot of trouble. And the more you talk, the more trouble you're lettin' yourself in for."

Doc Bigby smiled and showed all his teeth. "You're in for plenty of trouble, all right, Len. Soon's I get my saw sharp, you're gonna have a little cuttin' done on you. There don't look to be enough of that arm left to feed a sick cat."

Hawkins stopped his complaining and moaned. "Won't do you no good makin' noises like that, either," Bigby said. "Might make me nervous, might cause my hand to slip. You sure wouldn't want my hand to slip, would you, Len?"

Hawkins tried to stop moaning, but he merely succeeded in reducing the noise to a whimper.

"You go on and take care of the Moraleses," Vincent said. "Len can wait. Can't you, Len?"

Len whimpered in reply.

Later, when Paco and Mrs. Morales had been taken care of, Martha Randall took them home with her to rest and recuperate. Paco wasn't in any condition to be moved far.

"He's young, though," Doc Bigby said. "Tough. Hell, Sheriff, we were tough once.

You remember. He'll be all right."

Vincent explained to Martha Randall that Paco had nothing to do with Liz Randall's death, and Martha wanted to do something to help the boy and his mother.

"It'll help me get over what's happened," she explained.

She had come to Bigby's after being unable to find Rankin at his place of business, where she had gone immediately after watching her husband shoot himself.

She told Vincent about her husband's death. "I don't know why he did it," she said. "Just put that gun on his head and shot himself right there in the room. Maybe he was upset at the way Liz died. I don't know."

She did not mention what had been said at their last meeting, except to say, "I don't think he killed her, do you? Not his own daughter."

"No," Vincent said, "I don't think he killed her."

"I really think he loved her."

"I'm sure he did," Vincent said.

"Why would he do such a thing like killin' himself, though? I just can't understand why he'd do a thing like that, unless he was crazy. You think he was crazy, Sheriff?"

Vincent thought about what had happened at the Morales place. "Maybe he was," he said. "Maybe he was."

Chapter Thirty-One

When the stagecoach came, Lucille Benteen was ready to leave. Nothing her father said could change her mind.

"Things would always be the same here," she said. "You'll make Frank your foreman, and pretty soon you'll start thinking that he'd make just as good a husband as Charley. And maybe he would. But I wouldn't want either one of them for a husband. I know that now."

Benteen looked out the window of the hotel room. Things were more or less back to normal in Dry Springs. There were people on the streets, women in calico, men in sweated shirts, all going about their business as usual.

"What's wrong with Frank?" he said.

"Nothing," Lucille said. "Nothing that's not wrong with everyone in this town."

"What is that supposed to mean?" Benteen said, turning back to the room, looking at the packed bags on the floor by the door.

"It just means that a lot of people were ready to kill that Mexican boy for something he didn't do. Charley was one of them. Frank was, too."

She didn't say "You, too," but Benteen could sense that she meant it.

"We were wrong," he said. "We made a mistake."

"I know," she said. "And you tried to make things right."

She didn't say, "When it was already too late for Charley. And that gambler. And Turley Ross. And Len Hawkins. And the preacher."

"Sometimes things get out of hand," Benteen told her. "They go too far, and you can't stop them. I did what I could, there at the last."

"I know," she said, not mentioning that he had taken his men and ridden away, leaving the sheriff to work things out alone. "Can you help me with these bags?"

Benteen picked up the two heaviest valises. "Of course," he said.

"I wonder who did kill Liz Randall?" she said after they were in the hall. Benteen set down the valises and closed the door.

"We might never find that out," Benteen said. He took the cases again. "Not with that sheriff we've got."

"I don't know about that," Lucille said, starting down the stair. "I didn't think he had it in him to stand up to those men at the Morales place, but he did. He might surprise us again."

"Don't count on it," Benteen said.

Vincent found Willie Turner in the shade behind Danton's Saloon.

Willie was sitting with his back against the wall, his raggedy hat pulled down over his eyes. His mouth was open, and he was snoring noisily and wetly.

Vincent nudged Turner's foot with his boot.

Willie snorted and jerked in his sleep, but he didn't quite wake up.

Vincent nudged him again, harder.

This time Willie came out of it. He shoved his hat back and peered up at Vincent, but he couldn't make out who it was. He rubbed his face savagely with both hands, leaned forward, and looked again.

"Hey, Sheriff," he said when he finally recognized Vincent. "What time is it anyhow?"

"Time you were wakin' up," Vincent said. "You must've had a hard night."

"They're all hard," Willie said. His bloodshot eyes emphasized the truth of it. He was afraid that he knew what the sheriff wanted. He'd been trying to avoid him ever since that day at the Morales place.

"Somethin' I can do for you?" he said,

knowing the answer and dreading it.

"I need to talk to you, Willie," Vincent said. "About Liz Randall."

Willie sat up straight and started looking around him, as if hoping to spot a bottle somewhere. He had known this was coming, ever since that Benteen woman talked him into going with her. He hadn't wanted to go, but he had, and now he was sorry. Hell, that wasn't exactly true. He'd been sorry for quite a while, but he'd begun to think maybe he was going to get away with it, that the sheriff had forgotten about him.

He should've known better. Vincent hadn't forgotten, and now here he was, asking Willie what Willie didn't want to think about, much less talk about.

"I don't know a thing about that killin', Sheriff," Willie said, hoping that Vincent would believe him. "Except for what I've already said, anyhow. I've tried like hell, but I just can't remember, and that's all there is to it."

"I know that, Willie," Vincent said.

He didn't sound mad or anything, and Willie started to relax a little. He still needed a drink, needed one bad, but maybe it was going to be all right. Maybe the sheriff wasn't going to do anything to him.

"I was just hopin' to jog your memory a

little bit," Vincent said.

Willie leaned back against the wall and closed his eyes. He didn't want his memory jogged. Maybe if he just sat there, the sheriff would go away.

Vincent nudged his foot again. "Look at me, Willie. I got to ask you a question."

Willie opened his eyes reluctantly. "Okay, Sheriff. I guess you got to if you say so."

"I want you to think real hard, Willie. I want you to tell me who you saw that night besides Paco Morales."

"I told you I've tried to remember that," Willie said. "I can't. I flat can't."

"Try again," Vincent suggested. "I'll give you a little help." He told Willie a name. "Did you see him that night, Willie. Was he there in the grove?"

Willie was shocked at the mention of the name, but he was even more shocked to think that Vincent was right. Somehow the mention of the name had penetrated the alcoholic fog that surrounded Willie's brain and made him recall something that he believed he had forgotten or never even known.

"That's right, by God," he said. "He was there. He —" Willie started suddenly to get up, trying to get his feet under him as if he might run away. "He's the one done it! He's the one killed the girl!"

"You're sure about that, Willie?"

Willie got to his feet, excited now. "Sure I'm sure. I don't see why I didn't remember that before! He's the one, all right. He's the one."

"Tell me about it," Vincent said.

Willie thought for a minute. "Well, I went out there with a bottle. Maybe half a bottle. Sometimes I'd talk to that Randall girl, but not that night. He'd got there before me, I guess. Cut her up like that. I saw him cleanin' up as best he could, but he didn't see me. No, sir. I couldn't make out exactly what it was he was doin', so I waited till he left. Then I went and looked and saw that girl. I drank that whole bottle. Or half of one, whatever I had. Straight down. I never saw anything like that before, and I just slugged it all down."

Willie's face was white at the memory. "Then I got sick. Walked off into the brush and puked. Then I passed out, I guess. Didn't wake up till that Morales boy came by. But he didn't do nothin'."

Willie was sweating profusely. He wiped a hand across his forehead. "What're you goin' to do, Sheriff?"

"Arrest him," Vincent said. "You willin' to be a witness at the trial?"

Willie laughed ruefully. "Who'd believe me?" he said.

"The jury might," Vincent said. "What with the other evidence I've got."

"Well, I might be willin'," Willie said. "Maybe."

"We'll see if you're needed," Vincent said. "It'll be a while."

That was fine with Willie. He figured that what he needed right then was a bottle. Just one drink wouldn't do it, not this time. He looked at the sun. It wasn't too early to get started.

Vincent went to Doc Bigby's office. The doc was there, polishing his surgical instruments, and he was glad to see Vincent.

"The patients are all doin' good," he said. "That boy's got the constitution of a mule. He'll be out workin' on that little farm before you know it."

"That's fine," Vincent said. "How're you doin', Doc?"

"Me? Hell, I'm doin' good, too." Bigby's grin lit up the room. "If I was doin' any better, I'd think I'd died and gone to heaven. How about you?"

"Not so good," Vincent said. It was what he'd learned from Willie that was making him feel bad, he thought. He'd known already, but he'd wanted a witness. Now that he had one, he didn't feel any better about things.

"Got a fever?" Bigby asked. "Or is it one of those stomach things that's been gettin' folks down? If it's the stomach, I got a patent medicine here somewhere that's supposed to be the proper stuff."

"It's not that," Vincent said.

"Well, what is it then? You can tell me. I'm the doctor."

"It's about the Randall girl," Vincent said. "I know who killed her."

Bigby grinned even wider. "Well, now, that's just fine. You arrested him yet?"

"I'm about to," Vincent said.

"Who is the son of a bitch?" Bigby said.

"You are," Vincent told him.

Bigby laughed. "You always were one for funnin' a fella," he said when his laughter died down. His hand strayed toward a gleaming scalpel that was lying by his open bag.

"That the one you used on the girl?" Vincent said.

Bigby jerked his hand away as if the scalpel might have burned him. "I don't know what you're tryin' to tell me," he said.

"I'm tellin' you that you killed Liz Randall," Vincent said. "I know it and you know it, so you can quit foolin'."

Bigby wasn't smiling now. "I don't know what's got into you, Sheriff. You do need some medicine, I guess."

"I don't need any medicine," Vincent said. "You lied to me, Doc, and you left some things out that you didn't need to leave out. You killed her, all right."

"Lied?" Bigby said, seeming genuinely puzzled. "What did I lie about?"

"About that horse that foaled," Vincent said. "You shouldn't've told that story to explain why you looked the way you did that night. Too easy to check."

"You talked to Stuart, huh?" Bigby said. "Why'd you go and do a thing like that?"

"Because you didn't tell me the girl was pregnant," Vincent said.

"I told you that when you asked me," Bigby said.

"Not at first, though, and you knew it all along. Charley told me that the girl'd been to see you about it before she went to Miz Morales, and you didn't mention that, either. You should've told me, Doc."

"I didn't think it mattered," Bigby said. His voice was quieter than Vincent had ever heard it. "I didn't think you'd find it out."

"I did, though," Vincent said. "And then I got to thinkin' about it. I got me a witness, too."

"What?" Bigby sounded doubtful. "Who?"

"Willie Turner," Vincent said.

Bigby laughed again, but not with any enthusiasm. "Willie Turner," he said flatly.

"I figger it like this," Vincent said. "She was a pretty thing, and she'd been with a man. You knew that. So maybe you ran across her in the woods, saw she was alone, and stopped to talk. Maybe you tried to do a little more than talk, and she didn't go for it. Maybe you decided to put a scare into her with somethin' sharp."

"Lotta maybes in there," Bigby said.

"Yeah," Vincent said. "But it's pretty close to the truth, I bet."

"Yeah," Bigby said. "Yeah, it is." He looked at Vincent. "You don't know what it's like, Sheriff, people laughin' at you behind your back all the time. I know I ain't much of a doctor, but I smile and try to be likable. It don't do me any good, though, not a bit. I tried to be sweet to that girl, and she laughed in my face. It wouldn't have hurt her to be nice to me, would it?" His hand was straying toward the scalpel again.

Vincent pulled his gun from the holster. "Once was enough, Doc."

Bigby moved faster than Vincent thought he could, bringing up the scalpel with the speed of a striking snake and slashing at Vincent's face.

Vincent stumbled backward, firing as he fell. The bullet slapped into the ceiling, and then Bigby was on him.

The doctor was stronger than Vincent would have thought. He had a grip on the sheriff's gunhand, pinning it to the floor. He was working the scalpel toward Vincent's throat, though Vincent was trying to force it away.

Vincent could feel Bigby's hot breath on his face.

The scalpel pressed against Vincent's throat and sliced through the skin.

"I . . . didn't mean . . . to kill her," Bigby panted.

Vincent knew that he was not going to be able to overpower the smaller man. There was only one thing he could do.

He fired his pistol.

The bullet hit the wall with a crack, not doing much else, but the shot surprised Bigby just enough for Vincent to throw him up and back.

As soon as Bigby's weight was off him, Vincent pushed himself away and brought his gun up.

"It's over, Doc. Put the scalpel down. Maybe they won't hang you, just put you in jail for a little while."

"The hell they will," Bigby said. He jumped for Vincent.

He must have known he didn't have a chance. Vincent shot him in the chest.

He looked almost like Turley Ross as the

force of the bullet hurled him backward. The scalpel flew from his hand and made a shiny arc as it fell. It clattered on the floor as the sound of the gunfire died away.

Vincent sat there and looked at Bigby's body and the red stain that was spreading under it. He should have felt good now that it was all over, but he didn't. He felt sick at his stomach.

There was a pounding on the door. Jack Simkins had been making his rounds and had heard the shooting. "What's goin' on in there?" he yelled. "Open up this door, Doc."

Vincent stood up and looked down at Bigby's body for one last time.

"Doc!" Jack yelled. "Dammit, open this door before I have to shoot off the lock!"

Funny, Vincent thought. The doc looked like he might be smiling.

"Doc!" Jack yelled again.

Vincent walked over and opened the door.

THORNDIKE-MAGNA hopes you have enjoyed this Large Print book. All our Large Print titles are designed for easy reading, and all our books are made to last. Other Thorndike Press or Magna Print books are available at your library, through selected bookstores, or directly from the publishers. For more information about current and upcoming titles, please call or mail your name and address to:

THORNDIKE PRESS
P.O. Box 159
Thorndike, Maine 04986
(800) 223-6121
(207) 948-2962 (in Maine and Canada call collect)

or in the United Kingdom:

MAGNA PRINT BOOKS
Long Preston, Near Skipton
North Yorkshire,
England BD23 4ND
(07294) 225

There is no obligation, of course.